ONE DAY MY DUKE WILL COME

TAMARA Gill

COPYRIGHT

ONE

Millie Woodville glared at the Duke of Romney's back as he strode from the drawing room at her sister's new home in Surrey. They were here for a week-long house party before they were to return to London to start the Season.

Her parents, although, would not, having decided to return to Grafton to ensure their small estate continued to run smoothly. Not that they needed to be in London. With four of their five daughters married and matched very high in the peerage, her mama and papa were indeed well-situated.

"Why do you dislike the duke so much?" Paris Smith, her best friend since they were old enough to crawl about and get near each other, asked her.

Millie narrowed her eyes at the mere thought

1

of the man. "He is so opinionated and correct all the time. Have you not heard him speak? He knows everything, you merely have to ask him, and he will tell you that fact himself."

Paris chuckled, covering her mouth with her cup of tea before taking a sip. "He's deadly handsome, however, which does blunt the barb of his mouth a little. Do you not agree?"

That was true, much to Millie's annoyance. The man with his dark hair that looked as soft as silk. He probably washed it daily. Dandy's tended to do that sort of thing.

Not that she could call him a dandy, in truth. He was too masculine, rugged, and hard about the edges to be so soft. But it would annoy him should she call him that, and that was good enough.

Aggravate the irritating man.

Paris cleared her throat. "He seems to enjoy sparring with you a great deal, Millie. Do you think he does so merely to be near you, speak to you?"

Millie scoffed. "I do not think so. I have given him no indication that I ever wanted to speak with him or hear his opinions. Even when he does give them ever so often." Like their discussion today on the Kiplingcotes Derby and whether or not that horse race is the oldest in England.

Everyone knew it was, even though Romney

seemed to think because they raced over farm-land, tracks, and lanes, it was not the same as a real horse race such as The Royal Ascot.

Such a snobbish, ducal thing to think.

And how dare he believe that he knew which fashion magazines women read more than most. The man was chuckle-headed and needed to stop making a fool of himself.

"Where has he gone, do you know?" Paris asked, looking at the door the duke had disap-peared through.

"To have another bath, I'm sure. He's always so very clean, and he wears gloves. Do you not think that curious?"

"I think after smelling Mr. Thompson at last month's country dance in Grafton, hygiene should be the utmost priority for some men. I think it quite nice that His Grace smells so well."

"Sandalwood with a hint of lily, I believe," Millie said without thought.

Paris threw her a knowing look. Her lips twitched in amusement. "Have you made a study of it, Millie Woodville? Is there something more to your annoyance with His Grace that you're not telling your oldest and best friend?"

Millie laughed, shaking her head. "Of course not. Nothing of the kind. As lovely as he is to look at, and I will be the first to admit that I be-lieve his angelic features are striking, he's just so, so...vexing."

3

"Well, at least after this house party, you will not have to have anything to do with him further," Paris said.

"The week cannot come to an end soon enough." She clasped Paris's hands, squeezing them. "I'm so glad we're going to have a Season together and that Ashley has agreed to sponsor us both. We will have the best of times, and I will not be so nervous making my curtsy to the queen with you there."

"I too." Paris smiled. "It'll be the best Season yet, and may we both find love."

"Oh yes, that is the priority above anything else," Millie agreed. A love match as grand as her sisters had found. That is what she wanted, and nothing else would do.

TATUM CHANCE, DUKE OF ROMNEY, slipped into the bath, the pain in his hip excruciating after his ride out on the Blackhaven Estate earlier this morning. He had wanted to see the ducal estate for some years, but the duke and his son had been estranged. It wasn't until recently they had formed a truce, and the house and lands been opened up again to society.

A duke also, he enjoyed seeing what advances in farming other estates employed. Not to mention he valued overlooking the tenant farming homes, all of which looked in good condition, clean and tidy. It was what he wanted for his estate and would use their methods in keeping ahead of maintenance if it worked, which it seemed to be doing here.

His hip sent a sharp pain down his leg, and he massaged the joint, trying to alleviate the ache. The memory of why he was injured made his gut clench, and he pushed the recollection aside, not wanting to think of Eleanor or her unborn child.

It was his fault for his current discomfort. At home, he often used a cane to help him get around. Here, however, at the Blackhaven Estate, he could not. Not without gaining interest from others as to what was wrong with him, and he needed to appear fit and healthy, not some lame excuse of a duke who could not keep the love of his betrothed and their unborn child.

He certainly did not need to give Miss Millie Woodville any more excuses to hate him or poke fun at his abnormalities. What an obnoxious, knows-everything chit if ever he had met one. She had driven him to the point of distraction only an hour ago. The Kiplingcotes Derby being the oldest horse race in England indeed.

The woman was absurd.

He clasped the lily soap, scrubbing his hands and feet before letting the hot water soothe his aching bones. A bath always helped his soreness, and once finished, he would have a tisane and rest for the remainder of the day.

The muffled sounds of guests going to and from their chambers floated into his room. A piano played somewhere in the house, and laughter rang out now and then.

He had enjoyed his time here, seeing friends he had not since last Season, and it was good to see Howley happily settled with Miss Ashley Woodville. The sisters all, even the menacing one Millie, too beautiful for words.

If only the little hellion knew when to stop arguing.

How unlike she was to anyone he had ever met in the past. Eleanor never argued with him; for some time, he thought he had found the perfect bride to be his duchess. How wrong he had been. Women, he concluded the day he was humiliated in Gretna, were not to be trusted, even forthright ones like Miss Woodville.

The door to his chamber burst open and feminine laughter that he knew as well as his own filled his room.

"I'll change and meet you by the river," Miss Woodville yelled over her shoulder to her friend before closing the door of his room. Leaving them alone.

Utterly alone.

Tatum gained his wits and struggled to his feet, reaching over to a nearby chair that housed his towel.

Miss Woodville gasped, and he cringed,

knowing she had turned and had seen him. All of him. Every little naked part of him.

"What are you doing bathing in my room?" she accused, her wide eyes taking him in but halting when her attention landed on his cock.

"Your room?" he said, covering his dick with his hand and fumbling for his towel. "Are you sure this is your room, Miss Woodville, and you are not incorrect for the first time ever? I know it would be a novel thing for you to be mistaken, for you are always right, but there is a first time for everything."

"Oh, you're so irritating. It would help if you left and," she gestured to his attire, or lack thereof, "you need to cover yourself and go."

A point he was trying to achieve. Cover himself, that was. Leaving his room, he would not do. "This is my chamber." He stepped out of the bath, wrangling his towel about his hips and covering himself. He strode over to her if only to tower over the woman and intimidate her a little. Damn, she was pretty and alluring and righteous.

She glanced about, and he saw the sickly shade of gray her countenance changed to the moment she realized her mistake. "Oh, dear. This is your room. I must go before I'm seen."

She spun about and wrenched the door open, and both himself and Miss Woodville came face-to-face with Mr. and Mrs. Woodville along with Lord and Lady Bridges. They had traveled down from London, especially to support the Dowager Duchess of Blackhaven in her reappearance in society.

Mrs. Woodville gasped and promptly fainted at Mr. Woodville's feet. Without checking on his wife, Mr. Woodville's gaze alternated from his to his daughter's, clearly unable to fathom what was happening.

"This is utterly innocent, and nothing untoward has occurred, I assure you, Mr. Woodville," Tatum said, holding out his hand when both Mr. Woodville and Lord Bridges took a menacing step toward him.

"Papa, I entered the wrong room, that is all. I have not ruined myself."

A pain-riddled moan came from the floor, and they looked to Mrs. Woodville, who was coming to her senses. "Oh, my daughter. My precious Millie is ruined," she mumbled before collapsing a second time.

Lady Bridges bent down, helping Mrs. Woodville just as Lord Howley joined the fray and took in the scene.

"What has happened?" Howley asked, pinning Tatum with his unnerving stare.

"Miss Woodville entered my room believing it was hers as I was taking a bath. I have not touched one hair on her head. I promise you all," Tatum said again, hoping they believed him.

"She's ruined. My darling, most beautiful girl,

whom we all had such hopes for, is ruined," Mrs. Woodville cried into Lady Bridges' lap, who looked up at everyone, at a loss.

"Mama, truly, I'm not ruined at all. See?" Millie said, holding out her arms. "I'm dressed, and you know a woman cannot be compromised with clothing on," she said.

Tatum barked out a laugh at the absurdness of that quote. He would be more than happy to explain to Miss Woodville later that what she said was indeed inaccurate. A woman could most certainly be compromised while fully dressed, and the mocking glances of every gentleman present proved his point.

"There is nothing for it. You've been caught in Romney's room, and he is naked, and you're an unmarried woman of a good family. You must marry," Mr. Woodville stated, his tone brooking no argument.

"Marry," Tatum and Miss Woodville shouted in unison.

The room spun, and his life flashed before his eyes. This could not be happening was his last thought before his vision went blissfully black, and the crack of his head hitting the floor was the last thing he heard.

Two

Millie heard the thump behind her and turned to see the Duke of Romney flat on his back from fainting.

"Oh my," Lady Bridges gasped, and Millie could not tear her eyes away from the sizable manhood that jutted out between the duke's leg and spread towel. His fall had opened the fold in the cloth and bared all to see his impressive...well, impressiveness.

Oh my was right. Her breath hitched, and heat suffused her face, spreading all the way to her toes as she gained a better look at him this time. She had never seen a man naked before Romney. Was that what was hiding under the comfortable-looking breeches men wore all the time?

She bit her lip, her attention dipping to the hairs surrounding his sex, his thighs, parted by his fall. They, too, looked muscular and hairy. All his years of riding horses had certainly put the duke into good health.

Her father and Lord Bridges brushed past her, quickly covering His Grace before her father turned a stern glance on her. "To your room, Millie. We will come and speak to you in a moment."

Millie did not argue and did as she was told. There would be a way out of this mess. Her parents would not make her marry the duke just because she had made the error of entering his room by mistake.

She left the room and skidded to a stop at the sight of many of the houseguests, all of them having viewed her exit the duke's room. She hoped they did not look closer and see him strewn on the floor with nothing but a towel.

Oh, dear Lord, she *was* going to be made to marry him.

She recoiled at the thought, gaining the sanctity of her room, slamming the door shut on anyone who was watching. She was meant to have a Season in town. Be swept off her feet by her one true love and marry that man. She had always wanted to find love, in fact, her sisters may state she was the most romantic of them all. From what she knew of Romney, there was not a romantic bone in his body. Certainly not one aimed toward her. Millie paced her bedroom floor and stared out the window, her mind fraught with what she could do to get out of this mess.

How could she have made such a mistake?

She turned and looked at the locked door that separated her and the room that adjoined hers. How had she not known that the duke was staying in the rooms beside her own?

It was all Ashley's fault. If she had not married Lord Howley, Millie would not have been at this monumental house where she had muddled up her room's location.

A knock sounded on her door, and bidding them enter, her parents joined her. Their faces were pale and disappointed but not without concern. Her mother at least was back on her feet.

"Dearest Millie, what possessed you? How could you have made such a grave mistake?" her mama asked, tears pooling in her eyes.

Millie shook her head, unable to grasp how she had either. "I counted the doors incorrectly. I was headed upstairs to change and walked in just when the duke was climbing out of the bath. It was an innocent mistake and one that I do not feel I should be punished for."

"Come and sit, my dear," her father said, taking her arm and leading her over to a small settee near the unlit hearth. "There is much to discuss," he said.

Millie shook her head. "There is nothing to discuss. I will not marry the duke. I do not even like him." She gestured to the door. "You have seen us together. We do not agree on anything. He's too opinionated and knowledgeable, or at least he thinks he is." She paused. "I could not abide him, and my marriage would be miserable. I would rather be ruined than be forced to be his wife."

Her mother rummaged for her handkerchief, dabbing at the tears now running freely down her cheeks. Millie hated to hurt either of her parents, but she could not do what her mind screamed no to. Should they marry, they would kill each other before the first week was out.

"Neither of you has a choice. The duke will join us shortly, and he wishes to speak to you. He will do the right thing for you and our family as he should, and you will accept him, Millie. There is no other choice."

Millie gaped, stupefied. Married! To the Duke of Romney!

She swallowed the bile that rose in her throat at the mere thought. He was atrocious, cocky to the point of arrogance. However would she put up with him as her husband?

Forever.

This house party had turned into a nightmare.

"I do not love him. I do not know or even like the man. How could you force this on me when he never touched one hair on my head?

He did not kiss me. He did not lay with me. Nothing. I entered his room, realized my mistake, and left," she lied. Better that than say she argued with him about his room first before leaving.

"That you and Mama and Lord and Lady Bridges were in the hallway was unfortunate, but I promise, I swear on my life, do not take my Season away from me. Do not make me marry a man I do not love. My sisters are so incandescently happy. Please allow me to find my happiness," she implored.

Her parents stared at her with pity, and Millie knew what they were about to say before they uttered a word.

"It is done, our darling girl. You will marry the Duke of Romney, and in time we hope you will think more favorably upon the union than you do now," her mama said.

"He is not so very bad, Millie," her father interjected. "He's handsome, athletic, and you'll be the envy of every debutante in London when they hear you married one of England's most eligible bachelors."

"And if that bachelor does not give up his bachelor ways? I'll be cuckolded before our first married week."

"Millie," her mother scolded.

Her father's mouth thinned into a displeased line. "Let us hope that does not happen. I'm sure he will do the right thing and be loyal to you. He is, after all, a gentleman."

"From what I've heard of society marriages, that makes little difference," Millie blurted. "Please do not make me do this, Papa."

Her father shuffled his feet with unease. "It'll all be well, my dear. Your marriage will not be an unhappy one, no matter how it came about in the first place."

Millie shook her head. Not believing that for a moment. "I think all of this is utter bullocks," she added. "I do not like or agree to this. You must intervene and put a stop to it. Making a young woman marry a man merely because she entered his room by accident is outrageous behavior."

"And yet that is what will happen, and there will not be another thing said on the matter. You'll marry the duke and save your reputation. I cannot allow my youngest child to be ostracized by her friends. You deserve more than that, even if that means you must sacrifice all that you dreamed of, ensuring your survival in this world."

Millie swallowed the lump in her throat. All her plans, her debut to the queen, nights at Almacks, her wish to be courted, seduced, kissed, maybe from the man who would be her beloved, all gone, and just because she counted wrong.

Damn the Duke of Romney to hell.

· · ·

TATUM TAPPED ON MISS WOODVILLE'S door and smiled at her father when he opened the door to her room. The chaos in the passage he had woken to had ceased, and they were now alone upstairs to deal with this unfortunate mess.

A mess that Miss Woodville had created all on her own.

His gut churned at the thought of being betrothed. Not just to Miss Woodville but to anyone. After Eleanor's cruelty, he relished his solitude and did not seek to marry again. He had a mistress who fulfilled his needs. He did not need a wife as well. He had a happily married brother who was more than capable of ensuring the Romney line. He did not have to marry or breed like others of his ilk to keep the family line going.

Should he marry the hellion before him, all of that would be ripped away. He could not stand having another betrothed who did not care for him. And Miss Woodville would certainly blame him for the prickly situation they now found themselves in.

He followed Mr. Woodville and kept his eyes on the gentleman's shoulders, anywhere but at Miss Woodville. Not until he had calmed his temper at her atrocious mistake would he look at her again.

Silly little fool. How dare she trick him into a union between them.

He sat on a vacant settee and faced the Woodvilles. Well, perhaps she had not tricked him. She certainly seemed to think his room was hers. But that did not change the fact they would now be forced to marry, and as a gentleman, he would have to agree to the farce.

He cleared his throat, the words difficult to get out. Not that he had a chance to speak first.

"Who has a bath in the middle of the day anyway?" she said accusingly. "You had not long risen from bed, and you had not ridden out this morning, for you were being a pain all morning in the drawing room. So why did you have to have a bath, Your Grace?" she asked.

He gaped. What the hell. "Excuse me, but I may do whatever I wish in my room, including bathing if I feel the need. You were the one who walked into my room as if you owned it and then accused me of bathing in yours. You're the fool here, Miss Woodville. Not I, but I will be paying the price for your error, no one else."

"We shall both be paying for that mistake, Your Grace, for life, not just you. Do not think yourself the only one upset about this monstrous idea of us marrying. I do not want to marry you at all. In fact, I would prefer scandal and ruin over being married to you."

"That is not an option. For either of you," Mr. Woodville interjected, his tone stern.

Tatum glared at the chit who would soon be

his wife. She was a comely piece of arse, but she would be mistaken if she were hoping for a natural marriage. He had no interest in bedding her. No one wanted to bed Satan.

And the murderous burn in her eyes told him she did not want him anywhere near her either.

He sighed at the thought of his future, one he was once content and looking forward to vanishing before him, and all because some country miss couldn't count.

Fool.

THREE

T his was utterly ridiculous.

The following day her sisters, all of whom were now at Blackhaven Estate, volunteered to make a celebration of her upcoming marriage to the Duke of Romney.

Millie stood beside the duke, glass of champagne in hand, as Julia made the announcement to the guests, if any had not already heard.

"Thank you all so much for attending my darling sister's first house party as a married woman. And to continue with the merrymaking, our family is delighted to announce the betrothal of Miss Millie Woodville to His Grace, the Duke of Romney. We wish you both very happy," Julia said, lifting her glass.

Her family shouted congratulations, along with a few startled guests who had not heard what had transpired between them.

Millie sipped her drink, forcing a smile on her

lips when she craved to scowl and wail at everyone. How could this be happening? How could she marry the behemoth man at her side who took up too much space and air in any given room he inhabited.

His crystal glass clicked against hers, and she glanced at him, his mirrored fake visage giving her some peace. At least she knew in this absurd farce of an engagement, they agreed.

"Thank you, everyone," His Grace said in his usual deep baritone that had always made her wonder if he used that seductive tone with his lovers. Which, from all accounts, she had thought were many. Would he give them up, such a carefree lifestyle, now he was to be married?

Millie fought back a snarl. Of course, he would not. Their marriage was a forced union and certainly not a love match. He had no loyalty to her, and considering how they did not get along, it was unlikely he would ever grow any.

Should she try to beguile him to fall for her charms, he would see the false ploy that it was and most likely laugh in her face at the ridiculousness of it all. They had done nothing but bait one another since their introduction. Their marriage would be a calamity.

"We shall be very happy," he finished, and before Millie could say a word about it, he dipped his head and kissed her cheek.

His warm lips touched her skin but a moment. Awareness of the masculine, virile man at her side ran through her. He was tall, handsome, a catch to be sure, and he was to be her husband.

But there was no love. Not even like. What a disaster they would be.

The idea that she would have to share a room, a bed with the duke, had not been something she had time to think on. Would he expect her to change freely before him, bathe, and even sleep?

A man she disliked.

Whatever would she do?

Could she run away? Was there anyone else suitable for her at this house party who she could ruin herself with a second time? One who was much more palatable?

"You look as if you're scheming something. Care to tell?" His Grace asked her, his attention on her. Had he been staring at her this whole time she was thinking of things to do to get out of this hellish mistake.

"I wish I could scheme myself out of this room and house far, far away from you." She met his eye. "We cannot marry, Your Grace. We must find a way to bring this farce to a halt before it is too late."

He frowned, finishing his champagne before gesturing to a nearby footman for another. "And what do you suggest I do? Flee and leave you to the wolves who would eat you alive?"

"It is a disaster," she admitted. "To think that in a matter of weeks, we shall be residing under the same roof, within the same bedchamber...I cannot fathom such a situation. We must escape."

He chuckled, and she glared at him. Not seeing anything that resembled amusement in their situation.

"Weeks?" he said. "Try three days. Your father has suggested under the circumstances of our reveal, as it was, that it would be best that I married you sooner rather than later. They have settled on three days, two from now, so I suggest you pick out your favorite gown and have your attendants selected for we're to marry in the Blackhaven Estate's church by week's end."

A cold shiver ran down her spine.

This could not be her future. This could not be reality. Millie turned to the duke and could see from his stern countenance that he meant every word he spoke. "I'm not ready to be a wife, not to you or anyone who does not love me." Three days and she would be forced to lay with the man at her side. How was she to retire for the night and know that a perfect stranger would want to be with her intimately?

She had not even kissed a man. How was she to sleep with one?

"I'm not ready to have a wife either, so we're equal on that score. However, I do not see how we're to get out of this mess. Your inability to count has sunk both our ships, and we'll have to face this travesty and deal with it together. Forever," he practically spat at her, reminding her of her mistake.

Millie wasn't a woman who allowed emotion to rule her, but something in his words, the meaning and the awful, gut-wrenching idea of sleeping with a stranger, was too much. She set down her glass of champagne and left the room. She had celebrated enough for one day of her upcoming nuptials. Nuptials that felt more like she was walking to the gallows than a church.

Gallows, too, would be much preferable to marrying the duke.

Tatum sighed, having not wanted to be as harsh to Miss Woodville as he was. She hastily exited the room and he shook his head at the reality that faced them both. Their future was grim indeed. They both would have to get used to being together, being husband and wife, which may take time. A lot of time.

He had never ruined anyone in his life, and he wasn't about to start now with the sister-in-law to his close friend, Howley. They had to marry, and she needed to reconcile herself to that fact.

He set his glass down and went after her. They would have to come to some sort of agreement if the marriage would occur without a hitch or any more scandal attached to it.

He caught up to her, sneaking into the music room at the back of the house. He followed her into the ample space. The gilded ceilings matched the grand piano, which was just as elaborate. A harp sat next to a window, a perfect situation to play and dream if one wished.

She heard the snick on the lock and rounded on him. She faced him, hands on decidedly lovely hips, her mouth pressed into an annoyed line. He ignored the fact her lips were a beautiful, kissable shape.

"What are you doing following me in here alone? Have we not courted scandal enough?" She slumped onto a nearby settee, crossing her arms over breasts accentuated by her position.

Tatum inwardly groaned and joined her, this conversation was required before their animosity went too far. "Millie," he said. "May I call you by your given name? Miss Woodville seems too formal in the situation we now find ourselves in."

Her eyes narrowed, but she nodded. A small win. "Very well, so long as I can call you by yours, whatever that may be. I do not like to be the only one in this farce of a marriage to be so formal while you are not."

"That is understandable. My name is Tatum Chance, Duke of Romney, to be precise. You may call me Tatum if that suits you."

She studied him but did not answer.

"Now that we have that out of the way, we do need to talk of the situation in which we find ourselves. We cannot move forward until I feel a few matters that will arise after our marriage are dealt with."

"Such as?" she asked him.

"Such as how we will go on as husband and wife." He paused, thinking over his words. Wanting to be understandable without being too coarse for a lady. "Our marriage will mean that you're not ruined, and I'm not labeled a randy dog who could not keep itself in its own yard."

"Sums you up well," she quipped.

He frowned at her. "If I had wanted to mount you, I would have done it already, Millie," he said, enjoying the kiss of heat that blossomed on her cheeks. "But I do not want you to think that I want us to have a usual marriage. Or at least the same as your sisters have found."

"Go on," she said, her eyes cautious and assessing.

"We do not know one another, and it would have been unlikely I would have courted you with my intent on marrying you. The only reason we're here is because of an error."

"Which I suppose you wish to remind me of yet again?" she said.

"No," he said. "What I'm trying to say is that I will not expect anything from you. I do not want a wife any more than you want me as your husband. I know that most young ladies wish to pick whom they marry and love for themselves, and I am not that man for you. You," he gestured at her, "are not what I planned for either."

"You speak as if you never wished to marry at all," she said, eyeing him.

He heard no malice in her words, merely interest. "That is right. I have a brother who has a son and is currently my heir. I do not need to marry. But fate has other plans for us, and we're now bound together forever."

"And our married lives will be together when we're out in London, but apart when home. Is that what you're trying to say since you expect nothing from me?" she asked him.

"That is right. If we're to have any peace, not to bicker over different opinions on matters, I think this way forward is most suitable. We shall look to society as a pair who may have unconventional beginnings but who have grown to care for each other. But in truth, you may do whatever you like within reason, and I shall do the same."

"How very sad that all sounds, but I agree. We should know where we stand and step forward as we mean to continue."

He nodded, glad she was intelligent enough to understand his view. "I could not have said the words more perfectly myself."

She held out her hand to him. "Should we shake hands on the deal, Your Grace?" she said.

He took her hand, warm and small, into his and shook it a little. "You have yourself a deal, Millie."

"As do you, Tatum," she returned.

Four

Millie understood perfectly what the duke was trying to say. He did not find her attractive and never would. He preferred anyone else but her to be his wife. She ought to be insulted by his truth, but she was not. If anything, it was a relief. She was glad of their plan and truce. It would mean she could travel to London, have her Season, and maybe even have a little more fun than most since she would be a duchess, not a country mouse whom no one knew.

"I will admit that I'm pleased with our plan, Your Grace. It will make this farce of a marriage tolerable."

He nodded, his face grave. "I do hope we can be friends and pleasant to one another. After all, we will be married a long time."

All true, but there was one fact he had failed to elaborate on. He would not ask anything of her, so what did that mean when it came to having children? He had his brother's son as his heir already. Did that mean he truly did not wish to sire any with her? Ever? Or merely did not want to discuss such matters, not now at least. There was already enough tension between them, and maybe he did not want to create any more right now.

Heat blossomed in her chest at the thought of sleeping with him, merely to have children. She had always wanted some, two at least, but she had hoped the husband who gave them to her would be someone she desired and loved.

She took in His Grace. He was handsome, tall, and muscular. Her gaze dipped to his arms, his strong, wide shoulders, not to mention his hands were quite large.

A shiver stole over her at the thought of him touching her with his hands. Would his fingers be nimble in undoing her gown?

She could try to tempt him with her wiles, but the thought made her stomach knot, and it would never work in any case. She was not worldly enough to be irresistible.

"Millie? Are you listening to me?" he asked her.

Millie started, her gaze flying to his. "Of course, I was listening. I was merely taking in all you were saying," she lied, having not heard a word.

"I stated that I shall give you a monthly allowance of a hundred pounds. If you need more, merely ask. That does not include money for gowns or other fripperies that you may like." His mouth lifted in a small smile, and she could understand why women fell at this man's feet.

There was something about him that drew in a person. For all his brawn and good looks, he was not unkind. Not really. They may disagree on things, but that was nothing in the scheme of things. After all, he was a duke, and he could have told everyone to bugger off and forget about him marrying her and saving her reputation.

She supposed she ought to thank him... "If I have not said it before, I am sorry to have forced this marriage onto you, but I thank you for not letting me ruin myself through my own fault."

He reached out and clasped her hand, squeezing it a little. "You are the sister-in-law to one of my closest friends. I would not let you suffer such a fate."

"I would hope you would do what you are for me for anyone," she stated.

"Of course, but our nuptials' hastiness is solely because of who you are and who I know."

"Very well," she said, not wishing to press the point. "Where shall we live? I do not think I have even seen your house in London or heard of your estate." In fact, up until this house party, she had not known much about the Duke of Romney at all. Having met him here, and their instant dislike of each other, she'd not wished to acquaint herself further.

How ironic that they were now engaged.

"I have a house on Grosvenor Square and an estate in Somerset, Denver House. We shall reside during the Season in London and travel to Somerset for our break. Both my parents are deceased, and I have one brother who is away at present in Scotland visiting friends with his wife and son."

"What is your brother's name?" she asked, having not gained that piece of information when they had spoken of him last.

"Lord Richard Chance. A good and kind sibling. My sister-in-law is Scottish, and they spend a lot of time up north."

"I look forward to making his acquaintance," she said, wondering if the brothers looked the same or had similar attributes. Millie could not help but wonder what they would think of her and how his brother's marriage came about.

He nudged her. "See, Millie? We can speak cordially when we put our minds to it," he teased.

Millie stared at him a moment. "How will we go on in London? Will you continue your bachelorhood lifestyle, or will you be a faithful husband?" she asked, needing to know.

He tapped his fingers on his knee, thinking over her question. "It is a difficult situation. We're not a love match, and I have commitments in

London that have not ended merely because of what happened here." He paused, a thoughtful expression on his face. "If we loved each other, I would not seek comforts outside the marriage bed, but we are not that couple. In truth, we are strangers, and I think it is only right that I may continue with my life as I have been living it before."

The pit of her stomach clenched, and she swallowed the bile that rose in her throat. However would she survive such humiliation? "So you are telling me you wish to continue with your lover in London, a mistress, I presume, and you shall persist using her until we form an attachment?" she stated for clarification. "Which I should add will never occur since neither of us wanted the marriage to begin with."

He frowned and hesitated to reply. "You have made it sound very wrong, and you're putting words into my mouth. I never mentioned a mistress."

"But," she stammered. "I may be a country miss, but I'm far from naïve. You wish to continue to live your life as you were before, which means you wish to have your cake and eat it too." The thought of such a future weighed on her like a dark fog that would never lift. "I will be disgraced if you have a lover."

He shifted his gaze from her to stare out the window. "I decided some years ago that I would never marry. My saving your reputation will need to be enough for you. That is all I can offer other than friendship, and I'm sorry that may not be enough, but that is all I can give," he said, his words ringing with finality.

It was not enough, but then she no longer had the choice to decide. She was ruined if she did not marry the duke, even if that meant her life was ruined anyway, even if she did.

What would become of her?

"I think we have discussed all that we can," she said, wanting him to leave her alone. She could dwell in her despair much better by herself than with him sitting beside her.

"I agree. I will see you at our wedding, Miss Woodville," he said, standing to leave.

Her lip lifted into a snarl, but she could not find a rejoinder to His Grace's words. There was nothing left to say in any case. Nothing at all.

THEIR WEDDING TWO DAYS LATER WAS held in the Blackhaven Estate's private church, with a wedding breakfast held at the ducal estate straight after.

Tatum stood beside Howley and watched as his new bride, his duchess, went about those gathered for the house party and thanked them for their congratulations.

She was a beautiful woman, today more than

any other. Her light-blue muslin gown suited her complexion, darker than her sisters, as if the sun had kissed her skin a little longer than most during their childhood.

A little out of the ordinary, she had worn her hair mostly down, pretty white flowers threaded through her long locks, accentuating her hair's curls.

He had always preferred blondes, but something about Millie's long, dark locks drew the eye. Today she looked like a water nymph, visiting from the otherworld to steal men's hearts.

Tatum shook himself from the fanciful ideas, tearing his gaze away from his duchess, to anything else that was not his wife.

"Congratulations, my friend. If I know the Woodville chits at all, and I know one very well, I'm certain you will be happy," Howley said, his gaze locked on his wife, who stood across the garden in conversation with guests.

"You are content that you married then? I did not think I would ever see the day that the gaming hell rakehell, Grady Kolten, married anyone."

His friend laughed, sipping his wine. "Very true, but the moment I met Ashley, well, the life I lived before paled compared to the one I could have with her. I'm certain you will feel the same."

"Except my marriage was forced on me be-

37

cause my duchess could not count the rooms correctly and saw me naked as a babe."

Grady choked on his wine and laughed. "What did she think? I'm assuming her take on that was positive since you married her so quickly."

"That was her parents' idea, not mine," he quipped. "But I do not think she thought much of me at all. We have been civil to each other since we agreed on how we will get on as a married couple, but I cannot help but feel that will not last long. I'm certain to do something that will vex her, and I shall be in the dog house."

"Do not do anything that will vex her then," Howley suggested, grinning.

"She does not like or trust me. This marriage is already a disaster."

Howley threw him a disbelieving glance. "You could always convince her otherwise on your wedding night," Howley teased, wagging his brows.

"We have agreed to separate rooms and lives in private."

"You're not going to bed her? What is wrong with you, man?" Howley asked him.

Tatum thought about his friend's words, not quite sure why he would not either. Not really. But then, he had made a mistake in the past of giving his heart to another only to have it crushed and thrown back in his face. He would not be a fool for another woman again.

His love for Eleanor had been strong, and he did not think he had it in him ever to give another such power over him.

Miss Woodville may be one of the most beautiful women he had ever seen, but he had promised not to ask anything of her, and he would not.

FIVE

Later that evening, with the help of her maid, Millie stripped off her wedding dress, her best muslin gown she owned that she had packed for the house party, and slid into a shift her sister Julia had loaned her.

She stood before the looking glass, staring at her reflection. She was married now, a duchess, yet she could not see any discernible changes in her.

It was odd she was looking forward to her Season and all that it would bring only a week ago. Now she was a duchess, would enter society at the highest echelon and not partake in any courtship.

Not even one with her husband.

She could hear Tatum in his room, her maid having explained the door between their chambers was now unlocked.

Millie was not sure how she felt about that.

To know that he could walk in at any moment and see her. What if she were changing, or was indisposed, or worse, bathing as he had been when she had walked in on him?

Married they may be, but she was not ready for him to see her in any shape or form other than the fully dressed kind.

"Oh, Your Grace, you look beautiful," her maid, Eve, said, fussing with her bed and grinning at Millie as if she expected her wedding night would be a wonderful, memorable moment in time. If only the maid knew the real mechanics of her marriage.

"Thank you, but I'm only sleeping. I do not see what all the fuss is about," she said, slipping her warm shawl about her shoulders before sinking into a chair before the hearth.

There was no way she would cross the room to her adjoining door with her husband and seek him out. How odd that word was. Husband. And she now had one. It would take some time for her to get used to such things.

A knock sounded, and Millie watched as her maid went to investigate, only to see her friend Paris standing on the threshold.

"May I come in?" she asked.

Millie waved her inside. "Of course," she said. "Thank you, Eve. You may retire for the night."

"Thank you, Your Grace," her maid said, dipping into a curtsy before leaving them alone.

Another change in her life that she would need to become accustomed to. The title and curtsy were strange since she had never had anyone curtsy to her before in her life.

"Come in, Paris. I'm not busy." Millie gestured for her to sit across from her. She was glad of the company and needed a distraction from her mind. Would he expect her to consummate the marriage even though he said he would not? The thought made her blood run cold, and she would not do anything she did not want to, especially with a man who, up until today, was her foe.

"Your Grace, how strange but wonderful that sounds. No matter the circumstances that brought on this marriage, I am happy for you," Paris said, bussing her cheeks with a kiss. "And I hope that it does not mean we will not spend as much time together as planned. I'm so looking forward to London next week, so I too can find myself a handsome duke."

Millie laughed, shaking her head. "You will have little trouble finding a husband. You're too beautiful for words, and I have always been particularly jealous of your hair. Strawberry blonde, I have heard it termed, and I think it is just as pretty as that fruit."

"Perhaps, but what will you do now that you're a duchess? Are you nervous about tonight? I know you were not particularly warm

43

toward His Grace, although you seem to have formed a truce the last three days."

"We have laid down our swords. That is true," Millie said. "But for how long, I do not know. He said we do not need to consummate the marriage, and I hope he continues to feel that way. I do not want to lay with a man I do not know. Or one whom I often disagree with. I do not think it would be pleasant."

Even though the thought of Tatum stripping her of her clothes, his large hands touching her body in a way no one had before, left her all shivery. But more disturbing still, she wasn't entirely sure if that feeling was unpleasant.

Paris nodded, her face grave. "It's inevitable that you will have to be with him intimately, but there is nothing wrong in wanting to get to know him a little better first. You never know," she continued, "you may get along with him better than you do now upon further acquaintance."

Millie scoffed. "I doubt that, but we will see. He's my husband now, and I can do little about that. But there is one thing I wanted to ask you before you return to your room," Millie said, catching Paris's eye.

"Yes, what is it?" her friend asked.

"Would you like to come to stay with me now at the ducal residence in London instead of with Hailey? I'm married now and can act as chaperone as well as Hailey, and you are my particular friend after all," Millie accentuated.

Joy flooded Paris's visage, and she all but bounced in her chair. "Oh, I would love that so very much, Millie. I did not want to ask since you're newly married, and one never knows for sure what that will entail for you, but if you think it will be alright, I would love to stay."

Millie waved her concerns aside. "It shall be perfectly fine. The duke will continue with his life, as shall we. I may no longer be looking for a husband, but I can certainly find you one, and we shall have a jolly good time doing so. What say you?"

Paris came over to her and pulled her to stand, hugging her tight. "Thank you, Millie. Thank you for everything you and your family have done for me. I know I would not be here or about to enjoy a London Season without your help. You are the best of people."

Millie hugged her friend back. Paris was not the daughter of a land owner such as her papa, nor did she have any substantial inheritance. But she did have family in lofty locales now, which would help get Paris a good match.

TATUM STARED AT THE CEILING IN HIS room, listening to the laughter and the gossip of his newly minted wife and her friend in the adjacent room. He wanted to speak to Millie but would cool his heels in his room until she was alone.

He was not entirely sure what he wanted to talk to her about. They had agreed tonight they would not consummate the marriage, but they did need to toast their nuptials, something they had not been able to do due to never being alone since this morning.

Not that Millie wanted to be alone with him, and if he were being honest, nor did he want to be alone with her. But they were married now, and when they returned to London, he expected no gossip regarding his marriage to the youngest Woodville chit.

He reached down and rubbed his hip. Today his blasted joint had been particularly prickly, and nothing he had done had made the pain relent.

He heard the door close in his wife's room, and tossing back his bedding, he strode to the adjoining door, knocking twice before entering.

His steps faltered, and he felt as though he had been smacked in the stomach with a brick at the sight that met his eye. His wife, her shawl haphazardly thrown onto her bed, but it was the woman herself that left his mind dizzy.

He had always thought her beautiful, but now, dressed in a shift made of fine silk that was almost transparent, made desire, wicked and hot rushed through his veins. He reached out to the door, holding it lest he closed the space between them and kissed every inch of the goddesses' body she had been hiding all these days.

"Millie," he croaked, clearing his throat. "I thought we should toast our marriage before retiring for the night."

She nodded but did not move. He could not blame her. She was an intelligent if not opinionated woman, and she would have seen his reaction to her. He had never been a man who had been able to hide his emotions.

He knew she did not want to lay with him, and in truth, he did not want to in return. But by God, he had needs, and he would not push her from his room should she darken his door one day.

He was a cad thinking in such a way, but he was also a man, and she was now his wife....

Tatum returned to his room and poured them two glasses of brandy. When he returned, she had slunk onto her bed, her slim ankles and lean legs his to admire.

He swallowed, handing her the glass and tipping his crystal against hers. "To our marriage. May we not always butt heads as much as we do, and may we one day be friends," he said, meaning every word.

A small smile lifted the sides of her kissable lips, tempting him more this evening than they had all day. It had to be the silk shift she wore. Where had she fetched such a gown? Or was this what she wore every evening to bed?

"To us," she returned, taking a small sip.

Tatum downed his brandy in one swallow, needing the fortitude to return to his room and not seduce his wife to slake his growing needs.

He sat beside her, watching her. "I will not ask anything as we agreed, but there is one thing I think we should do."

"There is?" she said, finishing her drink and passing him her glass. He placed it on her side table before turning back to her.

"Yes," he answered. "I think you ought to let me kiss you."

Six

"Kiss you?" Millie gasped, standing. "How dare you ask such a thing from me when you promised you would not force me into a situation that I was not ready for," she said, her heart pounding loud in her ears.

She walked over to the opposite side of the room, as far away from her husband as she could.

How dare he ask her to kiss him. Granted, it was not as bad as being asked to be intimate with him, but they did not know each other. Not to mention they were not friends. Far from friends, in fact. Nor had she forgotten that he intended to rut about London as he had before coming to Surrey for the house party.

Even if she found him partially appealing and had thought to beguile him into loving her as an option to save their union, she was not ready for that. Not yet at least.

He held out a hand, trying to calm her temper. It would not work. "I meant no offense. I thought it may help us become friends faster than we are now. That is all. I'm not trying to gain anything more from you this evening."

Millie did not believe that for a moment. The entire time he was in her room, she had the distinct feeling he was up to something. He was a typical rogue out of London who thought any woman would be his if he merely clicked his fingers and wished it so.

"I'm sorry, Your Grace, but I do not want to kiss you, not tonight and maybe not for many nights to come. We are not friends, have rarely got along, and to ask me such a thing is absurd. Please return to your room and stay there. I may have unfortunately placed us in this situation, but do not make it worse by assuming that I'm pleased by the outcome, for I am not." She paused, taking a calming breath. She gestured toward the adjoining door. "I think we should remain in separate rooms with separate lives."

He frowned, watching her for a moment. She wondered what he was thinking. From his severe, startled expression, she could only assume he was less than pleased by her honesty.

"You are right, of course. I will retire and wish you a good evening." He strode to his door, his steps faltering on the threshold. "Oh, I forgot to mention that I was never staying the entire week of the house party. Therefore, as my wife, you shall be returning to London tomorrow with me. I expect you to be in the carriage by eight." His annoyance at everything that had transpired between them was easy to hear in his words. "Good evening, Duchess," he said, leaving her alone.

At last.

Millie let out a breath she did not know she had been holding just as disappointment stabbed at her that she would have to leave with him tomorrow. Her family would expect her to do as he wished, even though she desired to do the opposite. He was so very vexing, bossy, and arrogant. And a duke who ruined house parties by leaving early.

She slumped onto her bed, shaking her head. How dare he think she would kiss him. Maybe she could add delusional to her list of words that illustrated the duke.

Her list of many.

AS AGREED, MILLIE BID HER FAMILY farewell after breaking her fast with them the following morning. They promised her to be in town themselves by week's end, so she would not have to wait long before she saw them all again.

She sat in the ducal equipage, her carriage now, she supposed, and smiled at Paris, who sat across from her, settled and packed to join her in London. Her friend had been more than boastful of the velvet, opulently padded seats, not to mention the warm bricks placed on the floor for their slippered feet, even though the day was warm.

"By tomorrow evening, we will be back in London, the Season having already started, and we should be able to attend balls and parties just as planned," Paris said, smiling mischievously. "When do you think you'll be ready to attend your first event as the new Duchess of Romney?" she asked.

Millie shrugged, thinking on the subject. "I should think with the opulence with which we're now traveling, I shall be up for a ball the night we return. Although we must suffer one more night with the duke before we can let him scuttle off to his own devices and leave us be."

"You do not like him very much, do you?" Paris asked. "Will you not try to make your marriage as best as possible?"

"He came into my room last evening and tried to kiss me. A man who has made no secret of disliking me tried to seduce me merely because I am his wife, and he thought he had rights."

Paris cringed. "Well, he does have the right, but I understand your concern," she hastily replied when Millie glared at her. "He ought not to, but do you think he's trying to reach out a hand of friendship?"

Millie thought on her words a moment. "Maybe he is, and I may clasp it in time, but not yet. This is all too new and strange for me, and he is asking too much by trying to kiss me." She shivered, imagining his lips on hers.

The blasted man had even occupied her dreams, his deep, seductive voice whispering in her ear to be bold, take a chance, kiss him.

His chiseled jaw, straight nose, and dark, stormy blue eyes could seduce a nun, but not her. She did not fall for such outward beauty and certainly wouldn't fall for the charms of a man who disliked her until their wedding.

"So your marriage will be in name only. For a time a least," Paris stated.

"Yes," Millie said. She sniffed, her vision of her friend blurring. She swiped at her eyes, hating how everything had transpired. "I'm so disappointed, Paris. I wanted to marry for love like my sisters, but it would seem that will never occur now." She fumbled in her reticule for her handkerchief.

Paris came and sat beside her, wrapping her arm around her shoulder. "Come now. It is not so bad. And you never know, in time, you may find you and the duke are more suited than you first thought. He may be your grand love, and fate merely stepped in before either of you could realize that fact."

Millie scoffed but smiled. "I hope that is true,

and I suppose I have a lifetime to find out if that is correct." She sighed. "I think he has a mistress or a woman whom he sees more often than any other in London. He mentioned it before we were married, explaining how our marriage would work. I do not know what I think of that," she said. "I mean, I know I cannot ask anything of him. We do not love each other, but I also do not want London laughing at me because my husband all of one day is willing to make a fool of me before them all by straying from the marriage bed."

"A marriage bed you're not willing to lie in," Paris reminded her.

Millie groaned. "I do not know what to do or how to make this marriage work. How I wish I did not enter his room that day. My life would be so much better had I not."

"Well, that is done now, and you are the Duchess of Romney. Remember, people will look up to you, not the other way around. You are the pillar of society, no matter the mechanics of your marriage, whatever they may be. Do not let the duke ruin your Season." Paris squeezed her a little. "We're going to dance until dawn and drink until the room spins. We shall make our own fun, and remember, Millie. You now have the finances of the ducal title behind you. You may throw a ball yourself, and we can go shopping. We shall have so much frivolity. Just you wait and see."

Millie found herself smiling at her friend's words. She was right, of course. She had been melancholy over her situation, but it did not have to be so droll. She was a duchess now, after all.

Maybe it was time she used that esteemed title to her advantage.

TWO WEEKS LATER, TATUM SAT IN HIS office staring at the list of bills from almost all Oxford and Bond Street vendors sent to his address.

He flipped through the piles of parchment, his mind calculating the hundreds of pounds spent in a matter of days.

By God, they had only been back in London two weeks. How could his duchess have spent a small fortune?

Not that money was an issue for him or that he could not afford to pay for her new gowns, gloves, and whatever else she had purchased, but did she need all she was buying for one Season?

One bill from a milliner jumped out with its cost. 123 pounds for hats. He leaned back in his chair, shutting his gaping mouth with a snap. He picked up the small bell on his desk and rang it. His butler Edwards entered all but immediately. "You rang, Your Grace?" he said.

"Yes, can you send for the duchess? I need to have a word with her."

"Yes, Your Grace." The butler shut the door quietly behind him, and within a few minutes, without a knock of warning, his wife, the Duchess of Romney, strolled into the room as if she owned it.

Tatum looked up and swallowed the curse that almost passed his lips. Miss Millie Woodville was no longer the country miss from Grafton. Now she was a duchess, regal, elegant, and more beautiful than he cared to consider.

Their marriage was born out of necessity, but looking at her now, a woman he had little doubt other men were considering, made him rethink his absence from her life.

He ought to attend a ball or two with her to keep the gossip down and ensure no other lord decided to make her his paramour.

SEVEN

Her green gown, overlaid with silk tulle, shimmered in the afternoon sun. Her hips swung seductively as she walked across the room to sit before his desk.

Tatum swallowed the curse bubbling up inside of him. How had she morphed into such a regal portrait of herself? They had been married barely a fortnight.

He took in her features, rosy cheeks, lips full, a small amount of rouge upon them, making them even more desirable. She wore small diamond solitaire earrings and a matching necklace. He had brought his mother's set out of storage for her upon arriving back in London.

Diamonds suited her, and seeing her today, the perfect duchess, the many bills before him became clear.

"Good afternoon, Millie," he said, forgoing

titles since they were alone. "I suppose you're curious as to why I asked you to see me," he stated.

She sat perfectly still, back straight and hands not fidgeting in her lap. Next to her, Tatum could not help but feel the lesser of the two, which was surprising, for he was the duke after all.

She cast a cursory glance at his desk, and her lips twitched. "I can only assume from seeing the many bills before you that you wished to speak to me on my inflated spending," she suggested.

He glanced down at the many bills yet to be paid. "Do not think I'm here to curb your spending, for I am not. You may spend what you like, but I am curious as to why you continue to purchase so many gowns and hats. Do you not have enough already for the Season, or is there someone you're trying to impress?" he asked, not sure where his last question came from.

He frowned.

She chuckled. "We are attending a ball almost every night, and if not a ball, then there are excursions to Richmond, picnics in Hyde Park, the theater, so many events and I cannot possibly wear the same dress twice," she answered.

"And how is your friend Miss Smith enjoying her time in town? Are there any suitors whom I need to inform her parents of?" he asked.

"No one yet, but we have not been in London long. We have the masked Daniels ball this evening, which I'm hoping may secure a beau or two for Paris," the duchess answered.

Their conversation was stifling, nothing like the sparring they used to have. If he were honest with himself, he preferred the former.

"Ah yes, the famous Daniels masked ball. I will be attending also. Do you wish to travel together?"

She thought on his words a moment before shaking her head. "I do not think that will be necessary. I know you did not want to marry me any more than I wanted to marry you, and I do not want you to feel obligated to carry me about like a porcelain doll. I will not break. You may continue with your life as if I'm not here. That was the plan, was it not?" she stated, her words matter-of-fact.

Tatum did not like the way her words made him appear. As if he were the worst of men, forced into a marriage he did not want, and one who refused to act the gentleman now that he was living such truths.

And while he had continued as he was before his hasty nuptials with Millie, he had not visited his mistress.

But tonight, he would see her, for she would be an invited guest to the ball.

Lady Charlotte Beaufort would be one obstacle he could not avoid, even if he had been trying. She would have heard of his marriage and would be angry with him, rightfully.

Had he not told her that he would never marry before leaving for Surrey? What a liar she would think of him, not that it mattered anymore. Like it or not, Millie was his wife now, and he needed to remember that whenever he came face-to-face with the formidable dowager viscountess. He did not wish to cause embarrassment to Millie in public.

"We shall travel together, which I think is best. I do not want any talk of our marriage, and if asked, it was not forced by your family. I know your sister and brother-in-law have ensured me that what occurred in Surrey will not leak here, but one never knows. The *ton* has loose lips." He knew that fact from a disastrous, previous experience and did not want to have to live through another scandal not of his making.

"Very well, if that is what you would like." She raised her brows, watching him. "Was there anything else you wished to discuss?"

"No," he replied. "You may go."

She shook her head but stood. "Please do not dismiss me like one of your servants in the future. I know this situation we find ourselves in is not what either of us wanted, but it is what we have to live with."

Tatum cringed, his dismissal ringing in his

ears. "My apologies. I'm not used to having a wife under my roof."

"No, indeed not," she replied before flouncing out of the room, leaving the scent of jasmine to torture his senses.

LATER THAT EVENING, MILLIE STOOD TO the side of the Daniels' ballroom and sighed her relief at seeing Paris dancing with Lord Astoridge. Her friend was kind, smart, and witty, and she more than made up for what she lacked in dowry with her other assets. She would be such a good catch if only the men of the *ton* could see past the fact she was poor.

Millie sipped her wine, her sisters, all four of whom were in London, stood nearby. Still, it was neither their conversation on the latest *on dit* nor how Paris seemed all but in love with Lord Astoridge, but her husband, who stood on the opposite side of the ballroom, deep in conversation with the Lady Beaufort, that kept her attention.

The Dowager Viscountess.

She narrowed her eyes and fought not to grind her teeth. Was it any wonder that the duke did not pay her any attention. This evening was the first time he had accompanied her anywhere in London.

Not that she wanted him hovering about, but he was hers now, and she did not particularly like how the dowager viscountess looked upon him as if he were a sweetmeat she would like to gobble up.

Her sister Julia joined her, her attention moving across the ballroom to where the duke stood.

Millie noted her sister's contemplating gaze and could not hold back her question a moment longer. "Who is she to the duke? You've been part of this glittering world for two years now, and I understand you would know everything about it," she asked.

Julia's lips thinned into a displeased line. "I do not want to upset you, dearest. And what I know is rumor only. There is no proof, not of anything. And we all know London is full of false scandals and rumors this time of year."

Millie lifted her empty glass to a nearby footman and soon held a full one again. "If you know anything, I need to be aware of it. I do not want to be caught unaware by any meddling mamas or ladies put out by my marriage to the duke."

"Well..." Julia hesitated. "This is only a rumor, and please, do not react to my words. More than ever, my dear, you're being watched and judged, and if you're found too emotional, they will then be talking about you too."

Dread pooled in her stomach. Emotional? What did her sister know that she did not?

"That is his mistress, is it not? I know he has one, he said so himself, but I assumed it was a paid courtesan, not a widowed viscountess."

Her sister reached out and patted her arm. "There is no proof, remember. Yes, they are often seen together at balls and parties," Julia continued, pausing to stare at the duke. "But that was before he left for Surrey. He has not been at any events since your union until tonight, and I suppose the dowager viscountess would be a guest he could not avoid. I'm sure that is all their conversation is about."

"Really?" Millie said, her tone cloaked in sarcasm. "It does not look like he is trying to avoid her." Millie only just stopped herself from gesturing toward them. "Look at them. Their chests are practically touching, and I cannot work out where the dowager's hand is."

Heat bloomed on Millie's cheeks. What would people think of them? Here was the duke, in full view of his wife, flaunting his love affair with his mistress.

She. Would. Kill. Him.

Millie downed her wine and started toward them. She heard her sister call out, but she would not be deterred. She passed the footman who held more glasses of wine and procured another before pasting on the most contrived smile she could muster.

"Your Grace, introduce me to your friend,"

she said, looking the viscountess up and down with a mocking air.

The viscountess dipped into a curtsy but refused to let go of the duke's arm. Millie stared at her hand before meeting the lady's challenging eyes.

The duke cleared his throat. "Your Grace, this is the Dowager Viscountess Beaufort," he began, introducing them both.

Millie smiled, but the gesture felt more like a snarl even to her. "You seem to be having quite the conversation. People have been asking me what you're speaking of, so I've come to find out," she said, watching them both.

The duke stared, unable to reply, but the viscountess had no issue partaking in Millie's challenge. "We were discussing when we shall meet up again, Your Grace. We have not seen each other for many weeks, and the duke and I are great friends."

Millie chuckled, taking another sip of wine. "Oh yes, I was informed of such this evening. In fact, I was informed of many things."

Great friends indeed.

EIGHT

Tatum knew what Millie was up to, and he could not deny that a little part of him was proud she had such gumption to join in his conversation with Lady Beaufort.

But then, Millie had never shied from giving her opinions, and it was clear she did not like the viscountess or trust her.

His wife's gaze lingered on his arm where the viscountess held him, and he did not miss the narrowing of her eyes.

"I suppose you have not seen him for some time, and there is much to catch up on." Millie pinned him with an unnerving gaze that he had never seen on a woman before, but if he were a betting man, which he was, he would say she was furious at his being with her ladyship.

"He is married now. To me, if you had not heard," she added, her words layered with dislike.

"Oh yes," Lady Beaufort said, chuckling.

"Romney did tell me something about your marriage. Being as hasty as it was, I should think many were caught by surprise."

Tatum needed to remove Millie from this situation. Lady Beaufort was not known for being kind to those she did not care to know, and it was only understandable that she would not want to know his wife.

"Well, I'm happy you're no longer surprised." Millie's smile toward Lady Beaufort was chilling. "Now, do excuse us. My husband promised me this next dance."

Tatum cringed and stepped away from her ladyship. His ex-mistress's lack of retort enough to tell Tatum it was time to diffuse this situation.

He held out his hand to his wife, but instead of leading her into the next dance, he started for the ballroom doors, ordering his carriage in the foyer. The *ton* loved a good scandal, and he would not give them another involving him. Once in his lifetime was enough.

"I'm not leaving. My friend is still here, and I do not want to go anywhere with you, you cad. How dare you cozy up to your mistress before me at a ball and in front of all of London."

"You, footman," he called, gaining the servant's attention. "Inform Miss Paris Smith that I will have the Romney carriage returned for her when she is ready to leave."

"Paris needs a chaperone," Millie said, wrenching her arm from his grip.

"Your sisters can do the job as well as you, and we need to speak. But not here," he insisted.

The carriage rocked to a halt outside the residence, and he escorted Millie to it. She rounded on him as soon as they were seated, and the carriage gained speed on the Mayfair streets.

"While I understand that our agreement means that we will live separate lives, you will not embarrass me again in front of society. My sister had to tell me who that whore was draped all over you. Anyone who saw you tonight knew what was happening, and I was left looking like the poor forlorn wife watching it transpire."

Millie crossed her arms over her chest, glaring at him. He took a calming breath, needing to stop himself from strangling the maddening chit. "I owed Lady Beaufort an explanation, and this evening was the first time I had seen her since our wedding."

Millie shook her head. Her cheeks flushed red. "Did you tell her how our marriage came about?"

"I did," he said, seeing no harm.

"You are such a fool. She's a woman scorned if she believes your love affair is over, and now she can tell anyone who will listen how the Duke of Romney came to have a wife. If I hear a whisper of how I walked into your room and was caught there, I will know who to blame."

"You're being a fool. That will not occur. Charlotte will not say a word, and I have her promise on this."

"Charlotte? Really? Well," his wife spat, fiddling with the skirt of her gown. "If we're to be friends, as you call it, your association with that woman in public has to end. I never want to have anyone, not my sister or a friend, tell me what I heard tonight and watch that nightmare play out before my eyes. You would not like me acting with such little respect, but do not fool yourself if you think I will always act like a duchess. If you go back on your word, Duke, so will I," she warned him.

Tatum ground his teeth. He could see her point, but his speaking to Lady Beaufort was wholly innocent. He did not even want to think about how Millie would react should she know of Lady Sinclair and their failed betrothal. "I informed her ladyship of my marriage and that our association was at an end."

Millie scoffed at his words. "I do not believe that for a moment. You may have told her of your marriage, but she was certainly not believing that her sleeping with you was at an end."

"You, madam, sound jealous. If you want me to bed you instead, inform me so I can make a suitable time to join you in your chamber."

"I will never be with you." She stared at him with such loathing he wondered if they would ever have some peace between them. He did converse with ladies and engage in conversations. Was his wife going to react terribly each time she viewed him in discussions? It was one of the reasons why he had not wanted to become entangled with any lady looking to be his wife. Lady Sinclair had left him standing at the altar in St. Pauls looking like a fool. He had learned his lesson and swore never to give anyone the ability to hurt him a second time. Women were too incendiary and changeable. Millie and her sharp tongue certainly filled that opinion.

"We should never have married." Her whispered words carried to him from across the carriage.

"The conversation was innocent, and I shall not engage her again in public. Does that suit you, Your Grace?" he asked.

"But you will engage with her in private?" She stared out the window, and he did the same, not wanting to watch as she bit her lip out of frustration. "If you continue to whore yourself about London, where does that leave me? If we ever consummate the marriage and look to have children, what if I become ill with some ailment you have caught while whoremongering about the slums?"

The carriage rolled to a halt before their town

house, and their arrival at home could not have come at a better time. "I had a lover, Millie. One, not one of many. She was faithful to me as I was to her. I do not have the pox or any such disorder."

The door to the carriage opened, and he stepped down. His hip chose that moment to give way on him, and he stumbled, falling to the cobbled footpath below.

God damn it, could this night get any worse? He did not think so at that moment.

MILLIE GASPED AS TATUM STUMBLED AND fell to the ground. She jumped from the carriage and went to his side, helping him to his feet. "Are you well? What happened just then?" she asked, hoping he was not overwrought from their argument, not so much that he collapsed in any case.

The duke managed to gain his feet with her help, and she escorted him inside, leading him to his library. His steps were slow, and she did not miss the small limp he walked with.

"Did you hurt yourself more than you're telling me?" she asked. "You're limping."

"No," he said, waving her concerns aside. "I have a sore hip most days, and I'm more pride hurt than physically hurt." He paused as they entered the library. "Help me to the settee, and then I shall be well."

Millie did as he asked, hating she had lost her temper and they had argued. They were supposed to be trying to be friends, not enemies.

"I must apologize for my outburst in the carriage, Romney. But please, keep your associations with that woman out of my view. That is all I ask." She knew there was little chance of them ever having a happy, loving marriage, but respecting each other in this way would at least stop her from being laughed at.

"I will do as you ask, even though, as I said, our conversation was innocent."

"Except she hung from you like a cloak, and innocent it was not." Millie walked to the door. She glanced back at the duke. He was thoughtful-looking as he stared into the fire. Tonight had been a disaster, and she hoped they would not argue again as they had. "I will say no more on the matter, but please, for me as a friend, do not make me a fool."

"I will not," he said.

Millie left him, heading for her room. She poked her head through their adjoining door and caught the duke's valet in the duke's dressing room. "The duke stumbled this evening getting out of the carriage. He's in the library, but I think he hurt his hip. Perhaps a tisane and a warm bath will help His Grace," she said.

The valet bowed. "Of course, Your Grace. I shall prepare everything right away."

She rang for her maid, then washed her face and changed out of her ballgown.

As she sat before her fire, she could hear the servants preparing a bath in the duke's room before the sound of splashing water came from the adjacent chamber.

Worse was the fact that she knew what he looked like naked. She could, if she wished, step into his room and take her fill. Wife or no, she did not have the right after the awful row they just had.

And nor did she want to see him such.

They were in a marriage of convenience, one born out of scandal, and she did not want to see him naked again.

Liar.

She frowned, busying herself with her bedding and thrusting such absurd thoughts aside. Silly thoughts of how their marriage could be so much better, should he only allow himself to care for her and no one else.

NINE

Millie read all of one page of her book before she shut it with a thump and placed it on her bedside cabinet. Her husband made a lot of noise when he bathed.

She rolled onto her side, staring at their adjoining door. Until he was abed, she would not sleep a wink. She told herself it was because he was being so noisy, but in truth, something she did not want to admit out loud, the thought of the duke naked, soaping up his muscular body haunted her.

The day she had walked in on him had been a revelation and gave her a greater appreciation of a man's physique.

If only it weren't Romney whom she had appreciated. He was so up and down with her that she never really knew what he would do next. Asking her to kiss him had not been what she thought he would ask.

But then, maybe he was trying to get their marriage onto a sounder medium. God knew it was on a wobbly one right now. Not that she had been helping too much. She had been less than welcoming, and she needed to try to curb her disappointment and make the best of their odd situation. Seeing him this evening with Lady Beaufort had triggered a misplaced emotion, feeling very much like jealousy that was not founded.

"Blast it," Tatum hollered before a splash and thump sounded in the duke's room.

Millie flew out of bed, racing to the adjoining door, and entered the duke's room without knocking. "What is it?" she asked, looking to see what the commotion was about. The duke was on the floor beside the bath.

Naked.

Again.

Ignoring her racing heart, she went to him, reaching for the towel that sat on a nearby chair. "Here," she said, laying it over his waist and helping him cover himself as best he could.

He struggled to his feet, his dripping-wet body rising before her like Poseidon. He smelled divine, like sandalwood and man. The urge to breathe him in rose within her, and she thrust it away for the unhelpful thought that it was.

"What did you do?" she asked him.

He stared at the hip bath and then back at

her. "I slipped and fell out. My hip, as you know, is not as it used to be." He walked over to the bed and sat, and she followed him.

"Would you like me to ring for your valet or have another tisane brought up?" His hip seemed to give him a lot of trouble more often than not. "Have you hurt your hip in some way? You favor it quite often," she remarked, stating nothing that wasn't true.

He rubbed his leg as he sat on the bed, watching her. "I injured myself several years ago and received my wound then. I lost my seat on a horse, rushing and not concentrating and I fell. It has bothered me ever since. The entertainment we participate in during the Season aggravates it, that is all—no need to worry. You may return to your room," he said.

She did want to go back to her room, but something in the way he spoke of his injury as if it still pained him halted her steps.

"I have heard peppermint tea is good for aching bones. Would you like me to procure some for you? It may give you a little relief."

He raised a cynical brow. "Do not tell me that the independent, opinionated Miss Millie Woodville is going to help the husband she does not like," he teased.

She shrugged, not rebuking his claim. It was true, after all. Sort of..."No matter what we may argue over and disagree on, I'm not unkind. Of

75

course I would help you, or anyone for that matter," she said.

He reached out and squeezed her hand before letting it go. "I never doubted, not for a moment," he paused, "but about tonight at the ball. I did end my association with my mistress, Millie, and I apologize that you had to see that in such a public way. It will not happen again," he said.

"Oh," Millie breathed, not expecting him to be so sincere with his words. "So you're not going to take on another mistress? How disappointed the ladies of London will be," she teased half-heartedly.

In truth, the thought that he would be faithful to her, for the time being in any case, was the best news she had received since before walking in on the duke in similar circumstances back at her sister's estate.

"No, it would cause too much scandal, and I have had my fill of being the tidbit of gossip for the *ton*. Let them find a new scandal to keep them occupied."

She laughed but was unsure what he meant by such words. Had he been involved in a scandal in the past? "I'm sure they will." She smiled up at him and found him watching her. The pit of her stomach somersaulted at the hunger she read in his eyes.

He was still sitting beside her, naked but for his towel about his waist. His chest rose and fell in steady rhythms. Millie's attention moved down his body, reveling in his taut, sun-kissed chest. Her fingers twitched to reach out and touch him, see if he were as hard as she imagined.

"Do you like what you see, Millie?" His deep, primal baritone made her jump. She met his eyes and read the laughter in them.

"I apologize, but your body fascinates me. I've not seen a man naked before, well, before I walked in on you." She ran a finger down his chest. "You're so toned. How did you accomplish such a feat?" she asked him. Surely horse riding did not give everyone such spectacular form.

"I'm very active," he answered, goosebumps rising on his skin. She shivered. To feel him, to touch what had been invading her dreams, was a fantasy she had not thought would ever come true.

"Let me tell you, Tatum, I, too, am active. I ride horses, walk and dance as much as you, if not maybe more, and I do not look like that under my dresses."

His eyes darkened and burned with a hunger that gave her pause.

"I doubt that very much," he said, his gaze sliding from her head to her toes. "Take the shift you have on. It is so translucent that I can almost make out what lies beneath."

Heat suffused her face, and she glanced down, realizing she had forgotten her shawl in her haste to help him. She crossed her arms, shielding her breasts from him.

He chuckled, the sound wicked. "Oh, come now, Millie. I'm sitting here without anything on at all. At least you have a shift, even if it is sheer."

Millie did not know what had overcome her, but she did not like him laughing at her modesty. She uncrossed her arms, raising her chin in defiance.

"Better, Your Grace?" She forced herself to keep her arms in her lap and not to run away from his inspection of her.

His hands flexed on the bed, and she wondered what he was thinking. "You have a beautiful body." He reached out, running a finger across the seam of her shift, pulling at the laces tied at her neck.

Millie had never been touched in such a way before. Her skin felt like it was on fire, blood rushing to her head and pumping loudly in her ears. She longed for his hands on her, and yet she also did not. He was a cad, a man who, until tonight, had a mistress who was one of their social set.

He argued with her at every turn, but none of that mattered as long as he never stopped looking at her as he was. As if she were the rarest and most precious gem he had found and wanted, all to himself.

· · ·

Tatum told himself to pull his hand away, to stop trying to seduce his wife.

Wife.

He still could not fathom that Millie Woodville was married to him or that he was married at all after his disastrous past with Eleanor. It seemed only yesterday that his ex-betrothed declared her love for another before telling him the child she carried was not his, severing any affection he once had for her.

But here he was again, with a woman who drove him equally mad with frustration and desire. Especially when she came running to his aid as if he were a damsel in distress.

He was not. His hip was injured, but everything else on his body worked perfectly well.

"It is only fair that I get to feel your body since you're touching mine," she said, reaching out and laying her palm over his chest. Her touch, soft and warm, made his breath catch, and he watched, transfixed by her interest.

"You're so hard," she gasped, outlining the muscles on his stomach with her finger. "There are little rectangles of muscle on your stomach. How intriguing."

His cock twitched at her words, and he bit back a groan when the underside of her arm skimmed his there. After all, he was a man, and it had been several weeks since he had been with a woman.

But here was his wife, coming to care for him. Maybe his tumble had made her rethink her anger.

She had every right to be annoyed. He would be, too, if the situation had been reversed, but Lady Beaufort was in his past.

"I like that you are touching me, Millie," he said, the truth slipping from between his lips more easily than he thought it would.

A small smile quirked her lips, and she bit her lip as she ran a finger over the whisps of hair on his chest. "These are coarser than the hair on your head." The devilish finger slid over to his nipple, circling the bud and sending a bolt of desire to his groin.

"Your nipples are smaller than mine," she admitted and gasped, slapping a hand over her mouth.

He chuckled. "Perhaps you ought to let me view yours to determine if this is a fact or not."

Ten

illie had a choice to make. She could continue ranting at her new husband, fighting him at every turn, or she could try to make her marriage, unconventional as it may have started, work for the better.

There was no reason why she could not make their marriage a love match like her sisters.

When he wasn't trying to be wise, the duke was a man she could see herself friends with. They had started wrong and had continued down that road. It was time, for her sanity, that she turned them about and started walking in the opposite direction.

Without thought, Millie stood, clasped her shift at the hem, and dragged it over her head, leaving herself as naked as the day she was born. She fought not to bolt from the room at her boldness. She had never been naked in front of a man before. Even if that man was her husband. Would he appreciate the view she had gifted him? Would he want to touch her as she had touched him?

Millie glanced down at her breasts, inspecting her nipples.

"You see. Mine are larger than yours. I suppose it's because I'm made to have children while you are not."

The duke sat stupefied, his mouth open as if he were about to say something, and then thought better of it. He reached out, just as she had done to him, and ran a finger about her nipple.

A shiver ran over her skin, and goosebumps rose at his touch. Heat pooled between her legs and a longing she had never felt before thrummed through her body. She had anticipated reacting to him and his inspection of her, but something snapped within her at his touch.

A need, a long, pent-up want that had been dormant, burned to life.

"I like that," she admitted, as his finger gave way to his hand. He cupped her breast, plying it as she stood before him.

"I like that too," he growled, standing before his lips took hers.

Millie had never kissed a man before. In fact, she had never done anything as bold as she was right at this moment. His kisses left her reeling, making her feel as if she were floating on an invisible cloud of desire.

His tongue tangled with hers, his hands wrenching her hard against his body. His towel fell to the floor, and she broke the kiss, wanting to see him.

"Oh my," she said, his manhood hard and standing on end. "Does it always do that?" She ignored the heat that rose on her skin at having to ask such a question.

"Only when I want something," he answered, tipping her face up to meet his.

"What is it that you want?" she whispered, although she was certain she already knew. But could they consummate their marriage, be together as they had sworn not to? At this time, they were not friends. How they had come to this situation, she would leave to ponder later.

Her body ached in a way it never had before, and she knew that the man before her was the only one who could slake her needs.

His hands flexed on her bottom, squeezing her flesh and undulating her against his manhood. She moaned as his penis slid between her legs, teasing her aching flesh.

Millie closed her eyes, having never felt anything more delicious. She moved against him, wanting more of what he was taunting her with.

"I want you," he admitted.

He picked her up then and threw her onto the bed. She bounced once before he was over her, pinning her against the cushioned mattress.

Millie slipped her legs about his waist, and his manhood rubbed between her folds. The sensation was something she had never felt before.

His mouth took hers, stealing her breath and leaving her witless. He kissed down her neck, tickling her lobe with his tongue. His kisses were everywhere, working their way down her front, taking great pains in giving both breasts a thorough petting.

"We should not be doing this. We barely get along," she gasped as his tongue circled her belly button before dipping lower.

He chuckled, his warm breath tickling her skin. "Maybe this is what we needed all along," he said.

"What did we need?" she moaned. His hand dipped between her legs, cupping her cunny, his thumb making lazy, taunting circles upon her sex. This was too much and yet not enough. She wanted more of him. She coveted everything he could give her.

"A good, thorough fuck," he said, slipping a finger into her core.

"Tatum," she gasped, biting her lip to stop herself from screaming his name. She pushed onto him with a wantonness she did not know she had. He worked her, teased her until she dripped with need.

"I have to taste you," he said.

Millie yelped as his head spread her legs wider, and his mouth replaced his hand. "No, stop. You cannot do that." She lost all thought as his tongue lathed along her folds in one delicious swipe.

"Oh yes, I can." His words were muffled by her cunny.

Millie fought off the embarrassment and instead let him have his way. His mouth teased her sex, kissed and suckled, lathed, and pushed her toward a pinnacle she could barely wait to reach. Whatever he was doing to her was marvelous, dirty, and wanton, and she wanted more.

So much more.

She clutched his head, his hair soft under her palms, holding him against her as he continued his onslaught. She undulated against his mouth, working herself upon his tongue. Millie did not know what had come over her. How could she be so brave, so full of desire?

But she was, and it was Tatum who had brought her to this point.

How did she not know such pleasure was possible between a woman and a man? Was this why her sisters were always so incandescently happy? How had no one told her this was what she could expect in a marriage?

She had seen images in books in her father's library, but the images always depicted what appeared to be pain, not titillation. This, what Tatum was doing to her, left her breathless and needy, made her ache and long for things she had never known. She wanted it all. Everything, including his heart, if she could win it.

TATUM DID NOT KNOW WHAT HAD COME over him, but the moment Millie had stripped before him, the need for her overrode all their past hateful words, arguments, and petty disagreements, and he knew he could not walk away from having her.

Her sweet moans drove him to distraction. She was wet, dripping onto his tongue with her need, and he reveled in her excitement.

He had little doubt she had never come before and that he would be her first. Making her come at the touch of his tongue sent a frisson of heat licking down his spine.

He worked her, fucked her with his finger as he flicked her engorged nubbin. After their quarrel this evening, he had not thought their night would end this way, but he was pleased that it did.

Although he did not know what this change would mean for them in their marriage, at least in regard to sex, they came together well and could hopefully agree to do it again.

Her fingers clenched his hair, holding him against her as the first tremors of her orgasm clenched around him. She moaned his name, working her sex against his mouth. He did not relent, letting her take her fill as her release poured out of her like wine.

He came over her, kissing his way up her body, making sure to give each breast the attention it deserved before taking her mouth in a searing kiss.

She did not shy away from him. Instead, she wrapped her legs about his waist, crossing her ankles atop his arse. His frantic need for her proof he would not last long. He adjusted himself, teasing the opening of her cunny.

"Are you sure, Millie?" he asked, wanting to be certain.

"I am, yes," she breathed, trying to push against him and impale herself.

She would not have to wait long. Tatum reached down, lifting her arse, and thrust hard, once, deep into her cunny. She stilled beneath him, and he stopped, allowing her to adjust to his size.

She was warm, soft, and wet, and so God damn tight that he wanted to shout at how perfect she felt about him.

They did not move for several breaths. "More," she whispered.

He could not deny her anything. He thrust into her like a madman, and lust mastered his control. He took her like a youth who had never had a woman before.

Millie did not seem to mind. She held on to him, rocked with him, kissed him, her tongue tangling with his as they made a beast with two backs. This was no sweet joining that he ought to have given his virgin wife her first time. It was nothing of the kind. He fucked her and used her body to sate his own.

Owned her and gave her little time to catch even her breath.

"You feel so damn good," he admitted, having never felt so uncontrolled before, so at sea as he felt right at this moment.

She mewled in agreement, her words of encouragement as he continued his sexual onslaught of her pushing him forward.

"I feel," she breathed. "I feel as though I'm going to shatter again."

Pride rushed through him, and he liked that he would make her come a second time. He did not hold back in satisfying her. Her core tightened and spasmed about his cock, pulling his release forward.

"Millie, fuck," he groaned, forcing himself to pull out and pumping his seed onto the bedding as the last of their orgasms ripped through their bodies.

"Tatum." She stared up at him, her eyes heavy with desire. "I was not expecting that," she admitted.

Tatum nodded, catching his breath and understanding wholly what she meant. "Nor was I."

ELEVEN

The following morning Millie bathed and dressed early, wanting to stroll the back gardens of her new London residence and think.

There was a lot to consider. Last night and what had happened between herself and the duke were foremost in her mind. How had they been arguing like there was no hope between them and then end up wrapped up in each other's arms like they were the only two people on earth?

A shiver kissed her skin at the memory of what he had done to her. Of his wicked mouth and the delectation it wrought. How he had made love to her with such wickedness that she doubted she would ever look at him the same again.

He was so different last evening. Wicked and temping. Nothing like the husband and man she had known before whom she squabbled with at every turn.

She liked the different Tatum and wanted to see more of him.

Her body ached at the thought of having him again as she moved farther into the gardens and stole into a leafy area, secluded within several large trees.

If she were to win his heart, change his mind regarding having a wife, she needed a plan. It appeared her silk shift lessened his abilities to keep away from her, so that would be a point worth considering.

She had never seduced a man before in her life, but last evening, when she had bared herself to him, he had lost control and taken her into his arms, gifted her a night of unadulterated pleasure.

She sat on an iron chair within the gardens. But what to do about his past that still wanted to be part of his future? She narrowed her eyes, thinking of Lady Beaufort. Her ladyship needed to understand that she would not tolerate her overstepping her bounds with her husband.

She would like a husband who loved her, as her sisters had secured, and if that meant she had to declare her property and stake a claim on the duke, then she would.

"What are you doing out in the gardens? We have the Ridgehaven ball this evening. You don't want to be all red or freckly," Paris said from behind, startling Millie.

She chuckled at her silliness and patted the seat beside her, getting her friend to sit.

"I slept with the duke last evening," she blurted, hoping to be more diplomatic with her words but somehow not achieving that at all.

Paris let out a little squeal of delight, her eyes bright with excitement. "Tell me everything. I must know and live vicariously through you," she said.

Millie told her everything, how she had found the duke on the floor and assisted him. How they had both been scantily dressed and how they had ended up completely naked within minutes of her entering the duke's room.

"And he was pleasant throughout? You did not argue at all?" Paris asked, knowing their full argumentative history.

Millie shook her head. "No, not at all. In fact, he was so different from the man I married that one could wonder if he was the same person. But he is the same man and duke, and now I have a plan."

"A plan?" Paris repeated, looking at her with expectation. "What plan is this?"

"I wanted a love match for a marriage, as we all do. He did not want to marry at all. In fact, I do believe because his brother is married with a male child already, that Romney believes he will

93

do well enough to become the next duke. And that may be all very well, but it is not enough for me. I want the duke to fall in love with me, and now I know his weakness."

"His weakness?" Paris repeated, starting to sound like a parrot.

"Yes, his weakness is the indulgences of the body. As soon as I revealed myself to him last night, he pounced on me without a second thought. I want him to do that again. If I have to use that pleasant interlude to win his heart, then I shall, and I shall eliminate his need for his mistress while doing so."

Paris slapped a hand over her mouth, her eyes wide with distress. "Please tell me he does not still employ a mistress. Is that why you left early from the ball? Your sister, the duchess, mentioned that you were distressed and left with the duke."

Millie nodded. "I was distressed, for I was forced to watch him converse with her, and Julia told me of the rumors. We argued and left, but it wasn't until we were home and I heard a commotion in his room that I went to investigate. That's when it happened," she admitted, her body shivering at the memory of their first kiss. His hands as they pulled her against him. His wicked mouth.

How would she ever get through another day again and remain sane when all she could think about was him?

"He says it is over with his mistress, has been so before he left for Surrey, and I'm determined to keep it that way. I will not be the only Woodville daughter to marry a man who does not love his wife. He will love me, and I will win his heart. I promise you that."

Paris grinned, nodding in agreement. "I do not doubt it." She paused, her brow furrowed in thought. "We should return to the house. If you're to seduce your husband and win his heart, we have to look over what gown you will wear this evening. It needs to be both regal and flattering. Show him without being too evident what is his and what he can have, if only he wishes it."

Millie chuckled, thankful her friend supported her and was a little sinful as she was. "Let us go. There is not a moment to lose."

Tatum informed Millie and Miss Smith that he would be late in attending the Ridgehaven ball. Not because he was busy at his club. Or had a host of work to do left by his steward when he was away in Surrey. But merely because he needed to keep away from his wife.

All day he had caught glimpses of her about the house. Each time he had to physically stop himself from seeking her out, hoisting her over his shoulder like some neanderthal, and having his way with the chit.

She was maddening, and his cock still had not abated to its usual flaccid self.

The memory of her coming apart under him, her sweet cunny undulating against his tongue. He groaned. Damn it all to hell. How was he to keep away from her when he did not want to keep his distance at all?

He did not want a wife. Nor did he want to desire anyone beyond the norm. That path led to disappointment and broken hearts, and he knew that as well as anyone.

He waited for as long as he could before leaving the house and taking the short carriage ride over to Brook Street for the ball. His arrival, as late as it was, still saw him waiting in line as several other equipages dropped off their passengers.

While he enjoyed what had transpired between him and Millie last evening, he could not have the same happen again. He had promised himself never to fall in love again. To trust and be hurt, and he wouldn't start now, not even with the wife he had been forced to marry.

To give over his heart to his spouse meant she would have the power to hurt him, and he could not survive another such disappointment. Once was enough. He had been deceived into thinking his betrothed loved him as much as he had loved her. What a fool he had been. To know that the child she carried was not his and had been sired many weeks before he had met Eleanor still brought shame to him to this day.

He did not mind that he would be on better terms with Millie, but she could not ask more. That he hardly knew her did not help matters either, but he hoped she would not argue with him over the topic. His mind was made up. His future settled, and his new wife would have to fit in with those agendas.

He made his way into the ballroom, late enough that he was not announced. Tatum sought out the hosts, making idle conversation as he looked about the ballroom.

The room was a crush, and a smoke haze billowed above them from the gambling room and the hundreds of candles. Several terrace doors stood open, trying to cool those patrons affected by the heat.

He spied Howley beside his wife, with a besotted look on his face, and decided to join them. As for where his wife was, he had not seen her as yet, but she was here, somewhere.

"Howley," he called, coming up beside the earl and his new countess. "It is good to see you."

Howley shook his hand, clapping him on the back. The countess's acknowledgment was decidedly chillier than his friend's, and he knew the reason as to why and it did her credit to be wary. Millie was her sister, after all.

"I see you're out socializing in society once

more. It is good to have you back," Tatum stated, meaning every word. It was where his friend belonged, with them, not ensconced somewhere in the East End where no one ever saw his lordship.

Howley smiled. "You're late to the party. What kept you?"

"I was looking over some reports from Somerset and was waylaid. But I'm here now."

"And not a moment too soon. The duchess is quite popular this evening and gaining momentum as we speak. You ought to claim her hand before someone else does, and you miss out on a dance," Howley whispered, nodding toward the ballroom floor.

Tatum swallowed the curse on his tongue at the sight of his wife—comfortably entwined in Lord Fox's embrace as he spun her about the ballroom floor. That in itself was not what bothered him, however.

Her gown of rich, red silk, so dark that it shimmered almost ebony in color, was what made his senses evaporate. The neckline was scandalously low, the Romney diamonds dipping between her ample bosoms and keeping Lord Fox wholly occupied.

Before he knew what he was doing, his feet had started toward them. She would be the end of him. If last night did not do him in, tonight certainly would.

TWELVE

Tatum ignored the curious glances that came his way as he made his way over to his wife. Her laughter carried to him, and his swiftness increased. What was she doing dancing so close to Fox? From his lecherous appraisal of his wife, the cad was enjoying every second of her company and gown.

Fox would be lucky not to end up flat on his back with a bloodied nose if he did not stop ogling his wife's breasts.

"Duchess," Tatum growled, halting their dance and catching their attention.

His wife smiled, seizing Tatum unawares and leaving him grasping for purchase. She did not normally smile toward him at all. To be on the receiving end of her bliss was like being bathed in sunlight after years of living in shadows.

Not entirely untrue in his case.

"Duke," she returned. "You are a little early for our dance. The cotillion has not ended as yet."

He smiled, taking her hand and spinning her out of Fox's arms. "I'm sure Lord Fox will understand. Good evening to you, my lord."

Fox grinned at him, aware that his presence with his wife was noted and not appreciated. Tatum took a calming breath when Fox took one more appreciative glance at Millie's breasts before moving on.

Tatum continued the dance with her, trying to ignore how wonderful she felt in his arms and how annoyed he was that she had been in someone else's.

After last night they had fallen asleep, arms and legs entwined, only for him to wake in the cool dawn to an empty bed. To hold her again left him wanting her with renewed vigor. Something he had promised himself he would not do.

He would not fall in love with his wife. He would not be one of those fools who did. Never again would he allow the *ton* such fodder to make fun of him and his sensibilities.

"You're flushed, Your Grace. Is everything well with you?" she asked, her tone dripping innocence, but he could see the calculation in her brown eyes.

"If I'm flushed, it's because Lord Fox was all but ogling your breasts before the *ton*." He took in her gown, or lack thereof, and ground his teeth. Never had he seen a woman look more beautiful, more comely as his wife did at this moment.

He wanted to strip that evocative gown from her body and show her what rogues did to wives who were up for a little adventure.

"I must say I did detect that myself, but there is nothing in it. It's not like I'm married to Lord Fox and have to return home with his lordship. I'm married to you, and you're the man I go home with each night; therefore, you have nothing to worry about."

Tatum stared at her a moment. Her husky voice accentuated her seductive words. When had she learned to speak in that way toward a man? Surely she could not have become a Siren after one night in his bed.

Tatum noted who was watching them, displeased that most of the guests had taken an interest in his dance with his wife. "I do not think you should dance with anyone else but me from now on. We do not want to create talk, especially if it becomes known that our marriage was forced upon us as it was."

She shook her head, her defiant chin lifting. "I think not, Your Grace. I like to dance, and if you're late to arrive at whatever entertainment I'm enjoying, you shall have to learn to live with my slippered feet being waltzed about the ballroom floor by someone else."

"Do you enjoy dancing with other men?" he asked accusingly. He hated that his past made the jealous devil within him rise. He did not care if she danced with other men. His duchess could do as she liked.

He swallowed the bile that rose in his throat, conjured by that thought.

"As much as you enjoy dancing with other women." She met his eye and pinned him with a cold stare.

"I do not want you dancing with Lord Fox again. He looked at you as if he wanted to bend you over the nearest chair and have his way with you. Or eat you for supper."

She pursed her lips, pointing to a nearby settee that several matrons sat on to watch their charges. "Like that seat, Your Grace?" she mentioned, studying it. "Would I enjoy being bent over the chair as you suggest do you suppose? Even if it were Lord Fox who was the one doing such a thing to me."

He fought to control his temper. He wanted to pummel Lord Fox to a pulp, even if the rogue was not involved in their conversation. "If anyone is going to bend you over anything, it'll be your husband, Duchess," he warned her. The wobble in his voice ought to warn her that he would not tolerate being made a fool of again.

She lifted her hand, laying it against his cheek. "Oh, Romney, you should watch yourself, my dear, or people will start to think you're jealous and that you care."

He flinched, he did not want to care, but he would not be made a fool of either. They were completely different issues. "You are my wife, not anyone else's. It has nothing to do with caring or being jealous. I will not tolerate being cuckolded by my wife."

She glanced away from him, her mouth pulled into a mulish line. "And yet you had a mistress and may take another. And I'm supposed to accept that as my lot in life." She laughed, the sound far from amused. "I think not, husband."

"I do not have one now," he explained again. "That is what is important."

"If you want me to be faithful, Tatum, then you must be as well. What is good for you is also good for me. All's fair in love and war, as they say," she said, stepping out of his hold and sauntering off to the side of the room.

Tatum watched her and could feel hundreds of pairs of eyes watching his interaction with his wife. He did not care how they appeared, nor would he allow the conversation to end in such a way. She had to accept and understand marriage was different for men than for women. He had been jilted once, loved and lost, and he would protect himself at all costs. Even if that meant he appeared the biggest contradictory arsehole to live in England.

. . .

MILLIE FLED THE BALLROOM. SHE COULD feel the control on her temper slipping with each word she spoke with Tatum. How dare he think he could do whatever he wished because he was a man.

How unfair was a woman's life to be classed as lesser than a man simply because her sex was different from theirs?

She shook her head, unclenching her gloved hands while taking deep breaths. She strolled along a darkened passage and into a vacant room. The fire had long burned down, and only a few red coals were left to warm the room. She slumped onto a nearby wingback chair, thinking over her plan to make her husband so jealous that all he could think about was her. What she had been doing before he overtook her dance with Lord Fox.

At least she knew her plan so far had worked, even if he drove her to distraction by being such a neanderthal.

His obnoxious opinions would be hard to swallow or tolerate. How was she ever to keep her cool about him when he spoke with such little respect toward the female sex and their rights?

"Our conversation is not over, Millie," the duke said from the door, slamming it closed behind them.

She stood, hands on hips. "I will not be told by you or anyone with whom I can and cannot dance. It is beyond my control if the said gentlemen whom I dance or converse with admire my body." She slumped back onto the chair. "And anyway, I like a compliment here and there. They are nice to receive, you know," she said.

He ran a hand through his hair, leaving it on end. "Do not push me on this, Millie. I will not tolerate my wife sleeping with another man. I will not claim any children that are not mine, no matter how ruinous that may be to us both."

Heat kissed her cheeks, and she stared at him, wondering who he thought she was. The way he spoke, she could not help but think he thought her the worst harlot in London. "I have needs, husband. Needs that after last night you have awoken. If you do not wish for me to seek solace and satisfaction elsewhere, then you know what you must do." Millie watched him and bit her tongue to stop a smirk from lifting her lips. To gain his heart, to penetrate his cold outer shell, she had to do something, and right at this moment, the closest she could get to him was by sharing his bed. And she would do anything, even goad him into an argument, to get what she wanted.

His heart.

He swallowed, thinking over her words a moment before he started to rip at his falls. His large, hard cock slipped into his hand, and he stroked himself before her.

"Bend over the chair, Millie. Now," he commanded.

Millie gaped. "Are you in earnest, Your Grace?" she asked, having never seen him so discombobulated.

The hunger in his eyes and anger made expectation thrum through her. Her knees shook, and she clasped the back of the chair for support, bending over as he instructed. "Like this?" she breathed, gasping when he came up behind her, pushing against her gown with his cock.

"Yes, just like that is perfect."

THIRTEEN

Tatum wasn't sure what had come over him, but he knew he had to have her. Prove to himself if no one else that she was his and not anyone else's.

He teased himself, pushing against her silk skirts, reveling in the startled gasp of his wife.

She propelled back on his cock, seeking him as much as he desired her.

"I want you," she whispered, the profile of her beautiful face all he could see as she bent before him.

Tatum stroked his cock, hard and ready. He pulled her skirts up to pool at her waist. He could see all of her in this position. Her cunny glistened with need, and he did not miss her thighs pulling together in desire, showing him how much she needed him. She would get him.

All of him.

Every inch.

He bent over her, his cock slipping along her hot folds. He squeezed her arse with his hand. "Tell me it's only me that you'll be like this with. Tell me no one will ever make you come the way I do."

She rocked against him, reaching back to clasp his nape. She turned her head, her lips but a breath from his.

"It's only you I want," she breathed. "Only ever you."

Her words tipped him past his point of control, and he thrust into her heat, embedding himself to the hilt.

"Tatum," she moaned, her fingers spiking into his neck. "Again," she begged.

She was hot and tight, his mind fought for control, to not lose himself, to spend before she reached her gratification.

He cupped her mons, and she groaned, widening her legs and allowing him to touch her. She was willing and passionate. Never had he ever had a lover like her.

"You want me," he whispered, biting her lobe before suckling on it. "You want me to fuck you, do you not, Duchess?"

She nodded, sucking in a startled gasp when he thrust a third time.

"Yes," she answered. "I want you to fuck me."

Tatum gave her everything he had. He held her against the chair and claimed her body. She dripped on his hand, his finger teasing her engorged nubbin while his cock filled her from behind.

She mumbled words he could not decipher, but he knew what she meant and he could not refuse.

"Yes. Oh God, yes," she moaned. "Do not stop. I'm so close."

Tatum did as she asked. His balls tightened, and sweat pooled on his brow. He, too, was near, he could feel his release deep in his gut, but he held on. Wanting her to come first.

And then she did. She convulsed about his cock, dragging his own release along with hers.

"Millie," he grunted, his knees threatening to give way to the pleasure she wrought in his arms. He spent inside her, heedless of what that could mean. All he wanted was to join her in this pleasurable dance they both partook in.

She slumped over the settee, her arse in the air like a plump fruit. Tatum slipped free, kneeling down, and licked her cunny from behind. She tasted of come, his and hers. He spread her lips wide, lathing her sex with his tongue.

She shivered and moaned his name, and he knew she was on the brink of another orgasm.

He blew on her sex and watched as goosebumps rose on the skin of her legs. "Are you certain it's only me who'll ever see you this way?" he asked again.

He heard her groan. "Yes, now do not stop. Please, Tatum," she begged him.

Satisfaction ran through him, and he kissed her again, moved to suckle her nubbin and groaned when she came on his face, rode him without shame, heedless of where they were so long as she gained the thrill she sought.

"Tatum," she sighed.

He stood, shuffling her gown back down her legs and standing her up. She watched him, her eyes glassy with contentment. He grinned, glad he was able to satisfy her thoroughly.

"Did you enjoy our talk, Duchess?" he asked, reaching up to pin a loose curl that had slipped out of her coiffure.

"Yes, and I look forward to more of them," she said, leaning up to kiss him quickly before pushing past him and leaving the room.

He watched her go, slumping into the settee they had just used, righting his attire as he regained his equilibrium.

It would be some time before he would be suitable for society.

MILLIE WOKE THE FOLLOWING MORNING, stretching in her large bed, her body a little sore but satisfied after her dealings with the duke the night before.

He had been so angry with her, jealous if she

were any judge of character, when he had seen her with Lord Fox. But what he had done to her after their argument left her now aching for more.

Whatever was wrong with her that she could not get enough of him? He had started to invade her dreams and thoughts at every moment.

And if she could make him jealous again, whatever would his reaction be the next time?

Last night after they had been together over the settee, she had not expected him to kneel behind her and lick her to orgasm a second time. How filthy and wicked his mouth was.

How much she adored all of what he bestowed upon her.

She heard her husband's bedroom door shut and the sound of splashing, and she knew he was taking his morning bath.

She sat up in bed. Was she brave enough to join him? Would he welcome her?

Millie stripped herself of her shift, leaving it on the bed, and went to their adjoining door. Nerves pooled in her stomach. They had not seen each other again last evening, nor had she pressed his sensitive buttons further at the ball regarding other men, having decided to forego any further dancing. For that night, in any case.

She had not done anything to make him jealous this morning, enough to want to lay claim to her. But that did not mean he would not want her now. She certainly ached for his touch, more so each time she sampled his delicious body.

Taking a fortifying breath, she opened the door, slipping into his dressing room. His bathing suite sat just beyond, and she closed the space between them. She peeked around the door and noted he was alone.

Be bold, Millie. He will have you again. Just wait and see.

She stepped into his bathing room, leaning casually against the doorframe.

"Good morning, husband," she cooed.

He looked up, his eyes darkening with need, and she sighed a small breath of relief that he appreciated her effort.

"Duchess," he growled. "Are you wanting to bathe this morning?"

As calm and collected as she could muster, she came up to the bath, dipping her finger into the water to check the heat. It was warmer than she thought it would be and smelled of jasmine.

"If you have room for one more, I think I would be," she said.

Wickedness washed over his features as he laid his legs flat in the bath. "Come and sit on my lap, and I'll wash you," he suggested.

Millie did not need another moment outside the tub. She stepped into the water, straddling Tatum's legs and positioning herself against his sex. He was already hard, jutting up against her mons, and she moaned, wanting him with a frightening need.

They may argue and disagree over many things, but with this, the joining of their bodies, they were in total harmony.

He reached up, pushing her hair from her face. "It seems I cannot get enough of you, Duchess," he admitted.

His words filled her heart with hope. Her seducing him, making him feel for her, even if through sexual means, she hoped would reach his heart. To have him love her, to want only her. She knew she could be enough for him if only he allowed.

He just had to trust her. Trust in her, but for whatever reason, giving himself wholly to another was not an easy choice.

Why though? That was a question left for another day.

She grinned back at him. "Well then, that makes me happy, for I cannot get enough of you either. You and your wicked ways have left me wanting more, and I've become a wanton."

He growled, pulling her down for a kiss. His tongue tangled with hers, and their bodies slipped against each other, her breasts pushing against his hard chest.

Millie reached behind him, holding the tub as she positioned herself over his cock and lowered herself onto him. They moaned as she slowly impaled herself on his phallus.

He slipped a hand down her back, clasping her arse and helping her ride him.

In the warm, fragrant water, her head spun as his mouth, hot and demanding, took hers. His engorged cock filled her, and already she could feel herself on the tip of release. How could he ever think she would want this from anyone else but him? The notion was absurd.

He broke the kiss. "Fuck me, Millie," he said, leaning back to watch her ride him.

Millie sat straighter on his cock, watching him watch her as she moved on his manhood. So hard and long, taunting and teasing her sex with each stroke.

She clasped her breasts, rolling her nipples between her fingers.

"Good God," he groaned. His cock hardened further, and she moaned. "You're going to kill me," he breathed.

She chuckled, hoping not to go so far as that. "No more than you're going to make me crave you every moment of every day."

His hand slipped beneath the water, and he rolled his thumb against the sensitive part of her sex.

"Come before I do. I beg of you," he said.

The sound of his voice, his touch, pushed her over the precipice, and she fell into heedless gratification. Waves of ecstasy rolled through her body, and she rode Tatum, taking her fill, enjoying every last moment of her joy. Water splashed over the side of the tub, but she did not care. All she cared for was pleasing the man before her and herself in this wicked game they played.

A game she intended to win at any cost.

FOURTEEN

Later that morning Millie walked along Bond Street with Paris, their maids trailing behind them along with two footmen charged with carrying their purchases to the two carriages they had brought with them on their shopping expedition.

Millie played with the new kid leather gloves she had chosen to wear, a purchase from last week, her mind far away from the occupation with her friend.

Instead, all she could think of was her time with the duke. Their intimate joinings had become something unlike anything she had ever imagined.

Who knew that men and women could enjoy each other so? She certainly had no idea. Her stomach fluttered at the memory of their bath this morning. How she could not wait to join him again or maybe next time he would join her.

They came up to their carriage, and their driver opened the door, assisting them in climbing up. Millie smiled at Paris as they settled their skirts, her friend waiting for the door to close before she uttered a word.

"That is it. I cannot remain quiet a moment longer. You must tell me what is happening between you and the duke. At breakfast this morning, he could not keep from looking at you and the way he looked..." Paris waved her fan before her face. "Well, I'm surprised you did not go up in smoke."

Millie grinned and knew she looked like the cat who jumped into a bowl of cream. "We consummated the marriage again," she said.

Paris chuckled, shaking her head. "You cannot consummate a marriage more than once, but I understand what you're trying to say, and I'm happy for you."

"Thank you," she answered. "When we're alone like that, I feel so close to the duke. I'm hopeful that by making him passionate for me, he will open his heart and fall in love with me."

Paris reached out, squeezing her hand a moment. "I'm certain he will, for how could he not fall in love with you? You're charming and kind and passionate. Everything a gentleman such as the duke would want in a wife."

"Except he never wanted a wife. But I hope he soon reconciles that I'm here to stay and that

I'm not so bad after all. That I am, in fact, quite the catch." Millie chuckled at her words, glancing out the window to watch as they passed Hyde Park on their right.

"Your sister's ball is this evening. Do you know if the duke is to attend?"

"I believe so. He has not said that he will not, and she's family now, after all. It would be in bad form if he did not attend."

"And will you continue with your plan this evening too, Duchess?" Paris asked her.

Excitement made her heart beat fast. To think of them stealing away and being alone made her want the hours to pass quickly so she could seduce him again. "Of course. I will ensure my dance card is full and that I'm more than occupied should he not attend. But I'm sure he will, and with any luck, the duke will again not appreciate his wife being on the arm of any other gentleman but him and will soon put paid to anyone else stepping out with me."

"I like your plan, and if there is anything I can do to help, let me be of assistance. I want nothing more than my friend to be happy and content in her marriage."

"As do I," Millie answered. "I'm going to wear the blue muslin gown with the silver ribbon beading this evening. The duke left me a sapphire necklace and earbobs in my room. I think they will do nicely together."

"Nicely?" Paris declared. "They will look magnificent."

MUCH TO MILLIE'S DISAPPOINTMENT, SHE did not see the duke upon her arrival at home or the remaining afternoon.

"Thomas," she asked, handing a footman her pelisse. "Is the duke in his study? I wish to speak to him."

The butler shook his head. "No, Your Grace. He wanted me to inform you that he is spending the day at his club and will not be dining home this evening."

"Thank you," she said, pushing down her dismay that she would not see him before she departed for the ball. Still, she bathed and dressed for the evening. Ensured her maid did up her hair in the latest coiffure and threaded diamonds throughout the design.

She ought to make an effort for her sister's ball to arrive as the duchess she was, even if her husband did not attend. Paris, always by her side, accompanied her into Derby's London home later that evening, and they both greeted Derby and Hailey with a kiss and quick hug.

"I'm so glad you're here, darling. I want to talk to you soon, so do not disappear before I have a chance to catch up with you. It has been too long since I saw you last," Hailey said.

Millie could not agree more. "I will seek you out if you do not find me soon. I promise," she said, making her way into the ballroom.

No sooner had she stepped into the large, rectangular room was she swamped with gentlemen admirers who asked for her dance card.

She held out her arm, allowing them each to write their names for the different sets, pleased to see that Paris too had a bevy of men seeking out her hand as well.

"Come, there is a footman who has wine. Let's chase him," Millie said, linking arms with Paris as they made their way deeper into the room.

They gained their wine, watching as the many guests arrived before the first notes of a country dance started to play.

Lord Jessop claimed Millie's hand and escorted her onto the floor. He was a striking gentleman with a pleasant nature, if not a little elusive. Once she may have looked upon him with favor, but not anymore. Now that she was married and had been with her husband, all other men seemed to pale in comparison.

She only hoped that women paled in the duke's eyes also.

"I must offer you congratulations, Your Grace, but maybe condolences to everyone else since we will not have the pleasure of courting you this Season."

Millie laughed off his words, unsure how she should answer such a statement. "You flatter me, Lord Jessop. But, having been here some minutes already, I can see many young ladies who are more than suitable for those still seeking a life partner. I'm certain you will not be forlorn long," she said.

He grinned, his eyes sparkling in mischief. "But I do not want any of the other debutantes here tonight, or anywhere else in London for that matter. My interests lay before me."

Millie swallowed. She had never had a man ever talk to her so forward, not anyone other than Tatum. But she was married, the gentlemen knew that fact, whyever would he speak to her so.

Unless...

Heat blossomed on her cheeks, and she raised her chin, meeting his gaze. "Well then, I suspect you'll be disappointed with the ball, my lord. For my interests do not lay before me," she said, narrowing her eyes as she waited to see how he would respond.

He hurled back his head, his laughter ringing out loud across the room. "Romney picked well, did he not? But then, did he pick you, Duchess, or were you able to get yourself a duchess's coronet by underhanded means? A little birdy tells me that it may be the latter."

Millie fought to keep her composure at his lordship's words. Had someone from the house party told those in London the truth of her and the duke's marriage? Had Lady Beaufort, whom she had not seen present at the ball just yet, been gossiping about them as she suspected she would?

The laughter in Lord Jessop's eyes told her that was so.

"The little birdy that chirps in your ear ought to know better than to gossip. I will not lower myself to answer such a claim," she said, her tone chill.

He tsk-tsked her. "Come now, Miss Woodville. Oh," he gasped. "Do beg my pardon. Your Grace," he corrected. "But I never gossip. I only state the truth, which I'm certain you do too."

"Of course," she replied. Was he mocking her? When would this dance end? She wanted to be far away from this heinous man as fast as she could.

"What does it matter how you came about marrying the duke? You have his hand now and are the newly minted Duchess of Romney. It is a shame for us mere lords, however. I cannot steal you away if you're already married."

Millie could not understand his words, nor did she want to.

"You could not steal me away married or no, my lord. To steal one in such circumstances would mean one party would want to be captured, and I do not want to be captured by you. If you plan to continue to accost and accuse me of things I do not understand, I do not want to continue this dance."

His eyes widened, and he nodded ever so slightly. "I understand perfectly, Your Grace. I meant no harm or disrespect."

She scoffed just as the dance slowed to an end. "Somehow, I think now you are being untruthful, my lord." She did not bother to dip into a curtsy. Instead, she turned and left him on the dancefloor, certain he was more than capable of finding his way off to the side.

She joined her sister Julia who stood talking to Paris.

"Lord Jessop does not look pleased that you left him on the ballroom floor," Julia mentioned. "Is everything well, dearest?" she asked her.

Millie nodded, taking a deep breath to calm her racing heart. "He insinuated that the duke and I married due to scandal. I think people from Ashley's house party are talking and letting society know what happened in Surrey."

Paris gasped, and Julia looked to where Lord Jessop had last stood. "Do not worry, Millie. You're married now, a duchess. Few would try to slight you regarding how your marriage came about."

"But why would he mention it? Seems very odd, do you not think?" she said.

"Maybe he's jealous," Paris interjected.

Millie shook her head, not certain that was the case. "I think he wants to cause mischief more than anything else, but I suppose we shall soon see what gossip spreads about London. Then we shall know," she said, wishing that Tatum were here. He would know how to deal with Lord Jessop and how to calm her nerves over being the latest *on dit*.

FIFTEEN

Tatum dallied at Whites for as long as he could. He had dined with an old friend and had even traveled down to Howley's gaming hell to pass the time. Anything other than attending his newly minted brother-in-law's ball and seeing his wife again.

A wife whom he had become increasingly obsessed with.

His carriage rumbled over the cobbled lanes of the East End toward Mayfair. His putting off the inevitable long extinguished. He had to make an appearance and do his part for the family he was now part of.

A very powerful one at that. Even if the Woodville sisters had gentry beginnings, they were now at the top of society, and his marriage had helped them gain that privilege even further.

He had wanted to keep away from her today. It seemed whenever he was around her, he lost control of his masculine discretions and had to have her on her back at every chance he gained.

Which, from her eagerness, seemed more often than not.

What would he do about this chaos? They had not been on good terms when they married. They had rarely spoken before taking their vows, and yet now, all he wanted was to be around her, talk with her, kiss her damn sweet lips.

I will not fall in love with my wife.

Tatum repeated the chant in his mind, hoping that his very heart and head would follow the same rule. But something told him they would not. Whatever he had expected from their marriage was different from what he had gained.

Having Millie under his roof was enjoyable, not a bore. She was passionate, opinionated, and lively, all things he had been missing in his life.

And she was his. His wife and duchess.

Their newfound friendship, if that is what he could call it, suited him well, so long as she did not ask for more. He hoped she would not, for he would disappoint her.

To love and lose again wasn't anything he wished to do. To be made a fool for a second time, ridiculed and laughed at, was not to be borne.

He arrived well after midnight and missed supper. The ball was in full swing, the people merry from too much wine and frivolity. Tatum stood near the ballroom doors, looking over the sea of heads, trying to find his wife.

She was nowhere to be seen, and the pit of his stomach clenched. Perhaps she had already left, and he was too late to share one dance with her at least.

His steps faltered at the sight of Lord Jessop before he started toward him. "What are you doing here?" he demanded of his lordship, waiting for the blaggard to turn and address him.

As he did, the person standing behind him came into view, and Tatum felt the blood in his head drain away. He fought to school his features, to not give way to the boiling anger Lord Jessop and his late cousin's wife brought forth in him.

"Romney, darling," Eleanor, his former betrothed and now Lady Sinclair, cooed, using a seductive smirk that had once worked on him like a charm. But no longer. Now he saw through her veil of deceit she wore like a crown. "I had hoped that you would attend, but Jessop was not sure if you would. I'm so glad to see you again."

He blinked, dead to her charms. "I fail to see why you would want me to attend, my lady. We are not friends, have not been so for many years."

"Eight actually," she said, pouting. "You're not still angry with me, are you, Romney? I would hate it so terribly much if you were."

Lord Jessop chuckled and tried to cover his

amusement with a cough. "I suppose you're here to collect your new bride. What a charmer she is, the new duchess, and a very good dancer too."

Tatum ground his teeth, hating the thought of Millie in this bastard's arms or even around these two vultures. "You stay away from my wife, both of you. Do you understand?" he warned, his voice brooking no argument.

Lord Jessop held up his hands in compliance. "Well, here now, Your Grace. There is no need for you to be so protective of her. We mean her no harm."

Tatum did not believe that at all. Jessop was a backstabbing bastard who knew all along Eleanor was playing him the fool. Had owed Eleanor's future husband, Lord Sinclair money and, therefore, his loyalty too.

He studied Eleanor, so different from the woman who had left him standing before all their friends and family eight years ago, waiting for her like a fool when all the while she was miles away with Lord Sinclair, marrying him instead.

Eleanor sidled up to him, sipping her wine. "Have you told the duchess of your past with me? How we once were engaged?"

He narrowed his eyes on her, loathing her more than he ever thought possible. How he ever loved the viperish woman before him, he would never understand. How had he not seen through her lies? "Why would I tell her of you? You proved yourself less than worthy of my interest or thoughts. Do not fool yourself otherwise, Lady Sinclair."

She pouted up at him, and he pushed past them, unsure of what he used to see in the woman. To think he almost married her when she was pregnant the entire time with another man's child.

Never again would he fall for such tricks. His brother, happily married, could carry on the family name. He would keep Millie happy, just the two of them.

Millie was nothing like Lady Sinclair, he reminded himself.

Other than the fact she has stated, and not long ago, that she hated you. Did not want to marry you...

He cast his eyes over the throng of guests, seeing no sight of his wife. Noting the terrace doors wide open for the evening, he stepped out onto the terrace and found her.

Alone, with Lord Astoridge.

And his determination to keep her out of his heart grew.

LORD ASTORIDGE HAD KEPT MILLIE amused while Paris danced with Lord Flowers, not that her friend wanted to leave them alone. She seemed quite taken with his lordship, but the scotch reel was only a short dance, and Millie knew she would not be long.

"Miss Smith comes from Grafton like yourself, Your Grace? Does she have much family there?" Lord Astoridge asked, his eyes stealing through the terrace windows, which gave them a good view of the dancefloor and Paris whenever she passed them during her turn about the room.

"She is an only daughter. Her parents reside on the outskirts of town. We've been friends since childhood, and I care for her dearly."

Lord Astoridge nodded, taking in all that she said. "I must admit that I have started to think there is magic water in your small town, Your Grace. Everyone I have met so far seems very beautiful and pleasant of nature indeed."

Millie grinned up at him. Paris would be ecstatic when she heard what his lordship was saying, which Millie knew meant more for her friend than herself.

Did he want to court Paris? She would have to ask Tatum if he would be a good match for her friend and not some rogue who would break her heart.

An arm snaked about her waist, and she stilled before cool lips bussed her cheek. "Duchess, apologies for my tardiness," Tatum said, moving her a little back from Lord Astoridge.

His lordship bowed in greeting. "Your Grace,

it is good to see you. Your delightful wife was telling me of her home just now."

Tatum raised his brow, his eyes narrowing on Lord Astoridge. "Ah, she has spoken to you of her home. What a delight for you," he said. "She has not told me a word about it."

Millie frowned at Tatum. Whatever was wrong with the man to be so rude? She chuckled, trying to cover the awkward silence that followed. "Do not jest, Your Grace. We have spoken of Grafton many times," she lied. Now that he mentioned it, she wondered why they had not talked of where she had come from.

She supposed it was because their marriage was not one formed out of friendship and getting to know one another, but scandal.

Her mistake.

"Miss Smith is dancing at present, and Lord Astoridge asked me of our village," Millie stated. "Miss Smith will be back soon and will enjoy elaborating on Grafton much more than I, for I lived on a farm a little out of the township itself."

"I will have to ask her," his lordship said. "If you will excuse me, I shall go and see about a dance myself with Miss Smith."

Millie waited for his lordship to move out of earshot before she rounded on Tatum. "Whatever was that about? Why were you so rude to his lordship?"

"Because he was trying to seek your favors, and I will not stand for it."

"My favors?" She laughed. "Do not be absurd, Tatum. He is inclined toward Paris, not me. I was merely the vessel from which he gained his information until she returned."

Tatum scoffed, and she pulled out of his hold. "Stop acting like an envious arse. This is beneath you, and you do me wrong by accusing me of acting out with other men behind your back."

"I hope you are not making a fool of me. Each time I arrive at a ball, you're either dancing with some man or out on a darkened terrace deep in conversation. I will not be made sport of, Millie."

"And I will not be accused of things that I'm not doing," she spat back, turned on her heel, and left.

He watched her go, swearing under his breath before he followed her.

Sixteen

H e caught up to her, taking her arm and guiding her toward the exit.

"Where are you taking me?" she demanded. "I'm not ready to leave the ball."

Tatum was unsure what had come over him, why he was so uncomfortable seeing her speaking to the opposite sex, but he was. He supposed he could blame his inability to trust women on his disastrous failed wedding, not that he would suffer the same fate again, for at least Millie was his wife.

But that did not mean she would be faithful. He had never found women to be, even when he had given his heart. He had loved and still lost, and it left him with little hope for any future.

"Your Grace, do introduce me?"

Tatum cringed at the voice that called out before he could escort Millie out of the ballroom.

Damn it all to hell. Could this night become any worse?

His wife turned to see who called out to them and stopped to greet the unwelcome guest.

Tatum glared at Eleanor, and Lord Jessop, who watched Millie with a lasciviousness he did not appreciate. If the man did not stop acting like a leech, he would regret his choices by night's end.

"Lady Sinclair, Lord Jessop, with whom I believe you are already acquainted, let me introduce you to my wife, Her Grace, the Duchess of Romney."

To her credit, Lady Sinclair dipped into a curtsy, as shallow as it was, to his wife.

Millie smiled, unaware of who she was speaking to. Guilt pricked him that he had not told her of Eleanor or what had transpired between them. Another transgression in his past that his duchess would have to carry. Christ, he was a bastard who kept allowing his cock to lead him astray.

He was ashamed now for what he felt toward a woman incapable of emotion. Even now, as a widow, he doubted she could love anyone but herself should she marry again. That she had married the late Lord Sinclair was often rumored to be because of his obscene wealth. She had not married the man because she loved him, she only loved his money.

"It is delightful to meet you, Lady Sinclair," Millie answered, smiling at them both.

Tatum wanted to rip her away, remove her from people who were not fit to wipe her leather boots. They were not seeking an introduction to be friendly to his wife. If anything, they meant to cause her pain.

"And I you, Your Grace. I had heard the duke married and was keen to meet his new duchess," Lady Sinclair lied, all sweetness. "I was starting to worry that it would never happen for the duke, but I'm glad to see I'm wrong."

Millie sidled up to Tatum and linked her arm with his. Did she sense unease between him and her new acquaintances? Did Millie suspect she ought not to trust her ladyship and her charming words? She should not. For all of Eleanor's angelic features, there was a serpent lurking beneath her visage.

"We are very happy," Millie said, smiling up at him.

He smiled back, having not known his wife was such a good liar.

"How do you know each other?" Millie asked, turning back to Lady Sinclair. "This is my first Season, and I'm still meeting many acquaintances of His Grace."

Eleanor laughed, clasping her chest as if Millie's question had been the most amusing question she had heard that evening. Her eyes sparkled with mischief, and Tatum schooled his features, expecting the worst.

"Oh, well, that question comes with a long answer, one in which I shall allow the duke to elaborate. He is so much better than I at explaining things."

Tatum bestowed upon them all a benign smile. "I'm afraid that explanation will have to wait as we were on our way home. If you'll excuse us."

Before another word was spoken, he led Millie away, taking a deep breath of relief when they made the foyer.

Millie pulled from his hold, frowning at him. "Who is that woman to you, Tatum? You seemed less than pleased to be speaking with them again, even though Lady Sinclair appeared happy to be in your company."

He ran a hand through his hair. He wanted to leave, remove them both from prying eyes when they had this conversation. He looked around, noting only the footman who stood near the front door.

"Come," he said, taking her hand and leading her upstairs. "Where is the room your sister allocated to you when you were staying here?"

Millie started down the hall and led him into a dark, vacant room, the curtains drawn closed on the night.

"This is the guest room that I use," she said.

He closed the door, striding to the windows and wrenching the heavy, velvet curtains open so he could see her better without lighting a candle.

He leaned on the sill, staring at the gardens below, the people who milled about on the terrace.

"I do not want you interacting with Lord Jessop or Lady Sinclair after this night, and certainly not when I'm not around. They are not worthy of your friendship or your kindness."

He heard Millie come up to him. Her footsteps light on the Aubusson rug. "Why?" she asked.

He cringed, having never wanted her to know his shame. Or have to deal with his past, as messy and complicated as it was. The truth would only make their marriage harder, and it was already difficult enough.

"Because she was once my betrothed, and you should not trust her. No matter what she says," he declared, glad at least that he told her the truth and it was not something she had to find out secondhand.

MILLIE STILLED, AND FOR A MOMENT, SHE could not form words. Bile rose in her throat, and she swallowed several times, trying to find her equilibrium. Tatum had been engaged to Lady Sinclair. That his intentions toward the lady had been a courtship that the duke had wanted.

He had wanted to marry her, yet he had not wanted to marry her at all.

"Lady Sinclair is the widow of the Marquess of Sinclair. What happened to bring that about if she was betrothed to you?" she asked, unsure she wanted to know, in truth. Not when that truth had the means to hurt her heart.

Tatum did not meet her eye but continued to stare out at the gardens, lost in thought and the past.

"She changed her mind and married the marquess. That is all there is to know and all I shall say on the matter." He did turn then, sitting on the window sill and watching her in the moonlight.

"She is not a kind woman, do not be fooled by her sweet words or wishes for friendship. Please stay away from them both. Do not dance with Lord Jessop. He is Lord Sinclair's distant cousin and is loyal to his widow. They mean no good, and if they seek you out, it is only to cause strife."

Millie reached out, adjusting his cravat, which was askew. No matter the duke's cold, disinterested air, she could tell that he once cared for Lady Sinclair. As hard as that fact was to swallow.

Her heart clenched at the thought that he

had been hurt. Was that why he found it so hard to trust people. Her especially?

"I will do as you ask and not engage them more than necessary in society. I will not seek out their friendship."

He covered her hand with his, meeting her gaze. "Thank you," he said.

Millie did not know what came over her, but the thought of him being thrown over for another gentleman did not sit right with her. She stepped between his thighs, slipping her arms about his neck.

"You know, Your Grace, I find that we're quite alone." She grinned, playing with the hair at the nape of his neck. "Would it be scandalous of your duchess if I were to take advantage of the situation and kiss you?" she asked him.

His hands slipped about her waist, and she let out a yelp when he tugged her hard against his chest. His hands flexed on her bottom, squeezing.

Heat pooled at her core, and she squeezed her legs together, wanting him. She always wanted him. A madness that would not relent.

His mouth came down hard on hers. Their tongues tangled. She met his ardor with equal demand, the need for him pumping through her body.

He tasted of sweet wine, soothing her parched mouth and body that longed to be with him again.

He stood, broke the kiss, and turned her to face the window. His hands slid down her waist, cupping her mons through her gown. Millie gasped, reaching for the window to brace herself. It was cold beneath her palms, and yet his heat and body were warm against her back.

"Yes," she gasped, undulating like a feline looking for more pets.

He bit the lobe of her ear, his breath tickling her neck. "I need to have you." A statement, not a question.

She nodded, mewling when he wrenched up her skirts, pushing her legs farther apart with his.

His hand slid over her bottom, squeezing her flesh before dipping between her legs. She was wet, the ache between her thighs begging for release. He groaned, slipped a finger, then two, into her needy core.

She moaned, arching her back, seeking his touch. "Yes, Tatum. More," she begged him.

He removed his hand, and within a heartbeat, the thick, hard head of his cock pushed between her folds. She clasped the window, her nails scoring the paint.

"Take me," she pleaded.

He thrust into her, their moans mingling into the room. He was relentless with his taking and pushed her toward the diversion she sought.

Millie reached up behind her, clasping his

nape, tipping her head, and reveling in the feel of his tongue, his lips scoring her neck.

He owned her, took her, drove her toward ecstasy, and she could not get there fast enough.

"I'm going to come," she gasped, lost in his feel, his heavy, hard manhood filling her need with every stroke.

Tremors ricocheted through her core and out to every surface of her body. She screamed his name and rode him through her pleasure.

He groaned as he, too, found release.

They stood locked together, the ball in full swing in the rooms beneath them, the terrace that was within view. The sounds of a minuet floating into the room, and yet, Tatum's breathlessness was music to her ears. The only entertainment she fancied.

Tonight and always.

SEVENTEEN

The following morning Millie broke her fast in the breakfast room, her friend Paris seated across from her and grinning at Millie as if she knew something she did not.

Tatum sat at the head of the table, a paper before his face and obscuring her view of him. They had returned to the ball last evening after their discussion in the upstairs bedroom and had danced twice before returning home.

She had thought they would retire to their rooms to sleep. How deliciously wrong she had been. Instead, they had made love throughout the night. His kisses, even now, made her blood run hot and her body ache with renewed need.

She picked at the eggs on her plate, no longer hungry, not for food in any case.

Tatum sighed, folding the paper and placing it on the side of his setting. "I have business to attend to today. Have a lovely day, ladies," he said, standing.

Millie caught his eye, and his lips lifted into a knowing smirk.

Was he too thinking about last evening and everything he had done to her?

He walked from the room, and she followed his progress, enjoying the view of his muscular thighs and strong shoulders.

"Careful, dearest friend, or I shall have to declare that you're falling in love with your husband," Paris teased, sipping her tea, her eyes alight with laughter.

Millie shushed her but smiled. "Do not say such a heinous thing. How could I love a man whom I barely know and have fought with from the very moment I met him?" she asked her, the sinking feeling in the pit of her stomach telling her that maybe her friend had a point.

Was she falling in love with Tatum?

Or was she already in love?

Paris cast a glance in the direction the duke had walked. "I would think it very easy to fall in love with a man who looked like His Grace, and you have been getting along much better."

Millie frowned, thinking over Paris's words. "That is true, but he's very uncertain. Last evening he chastised me over being outside with Lord Astoridge, whom we all know is after another young lady from Grafton and one who is certainly not me."

Paris's cheeks darkened to a deep shade of pink. "I hope you're not insinuating that Lord Astoridge is seeking my affection?"

Millie laughed. "Admit it, friend, he danced with you twice, and his eyes followed you about most of the evening. In fact, when he was with me on the terrace, all he did was ask me of you. I think my summarization is correct."

Paris shrugged, biting into her ham. "We do not know that for sure. He may have merely been polite, and in any case, it is not Lord Astoridge who we're speaking of. We're talking of the duke and if your feelings for His Grace have changed."

Millie could not look at her friend. Her penetrative eyes had always been able to read her like a book, and she did not want to give Paris or herself hope for something she was not certain of herself.

"Let me say that my plan to be intimate with the duke is working, and I feel we're growing closer. But he has not declared any feelings beyond that."

"They will come. He certainly attends more events now, if you had not noticed. I think he wants to be around you, which I hope is a sign that he cares for you more than he once did."

Millie chewed her bottom lip. That was certainly true too. But was his attendance due to his growing emotional attraction, or merely because he did not trust her to be faithful? To not make a fool of him.

Lady Sinclair had once been his betrothed but had married another.

For Tatum to be engaged to the woman meant he cared for Lady Sinclair, more so possibly than he ever cared for her. Was he still hurt by the pain she inflicted? He did not trust Millie, that she knew above anything else, even when she gave him no cause to think so.

"I will continue trying to reach his heart through spending more time with him, but I feel he does not trust me, and I'm not hopeful that he ever will."

"You will prove to him, by your loyalty, that he is wrong and has nothing to fear. You will see, my dear. You too will gain a love match, even if it is hard-won."

Millie nodded. "I hope you are right. I will not stop trying until there is no hope."

TATUM LEANED BACK IN HIS CHAIR before his desk and stared at the door. He could hear the muffled conversation of Millie and Miss Smith in the breakfast room, although he could not make out what exactly they spoke.

But he could guess and be correct in surmising they were talking of him.

Not that he could blame his wife. He tapped his fingers atop the mahogany desk, the memory of their time together last evening alive and taunting his mind.

Had Miss Smith not been in the breakfast room this morning, he knew he would have dismissed his staff and had Millie atop the table, taking his fill, and enjoying every appetizing thing about his wife.

He was not sure when he had become smitten with her, but he was. He could not stop thinking of her. What she was doing. Who was she with. Whose company she kept at balls and parties he was not attending.

He rubbed a hand over his jaw. However would he keep himself from her when he did not want to? He wasn't supposed to care for her. Damn it, they had not even been friends prior to their wedding, and yet now, it was all different.

Being with her intimately did not help either. He ought to stay away, had told himself to do so to keep his heart safe from future hurt.

Could he trust Millie not to play him the fool as his last love had done to him?

Love?

Tatum stilled as the word reverberated in his mind just as a light knock sounded on the door and Millie entered his library.

"Do you have a moment?" she asked, coming

into the room without waiting for a reply and closing the door.

He cleared his throat, adjusting his seat, determined not to touch her again.

"Is something troubling you?" he asked her.

"No, not particularly. I just wanted to come and ask if you would like to join me. I'm going to go riding this afternoon in the park."

She sat in the chair before the desk, her light-pink morning gown accentuating a figure he had come to adore. She did not need such pretty fripperies as clothes. She was already beautiful.

"I would like that, yes. I shall have the horses prepared after lunch if that suits?" he stated.

"I love to ride and feel like I have not done it enough since I came up to town for the Season." She stood, strolling around his desk, picking up his quill and his paperweight, studying each item before placing them back down.

"I'm glad that we're becoming friends, and our marriage is not as argumentative as it first was. It seems that you're not so bad after all," she said, coming to a halt before him.

So perhaps she had been thinking similarly to him.

Without thinking, he reached for her, pulling her onto his lap. Forgetting his rule not to continue touching his wife. "I, too, am glad that we're friends," he stated, knowing how underwhelming that sounded. Friends, such a benign statement. What he felt for the woman in his arms was far more than that.

And that in itself terrified him.

What if she hurt him too? What if he had unwillingly given her his heart, yet she did not want it? Not really. There was a chance she only wanted his attention in bed and nothing else.

"I did not like that we argued all the time," he admitted, pushing a lock of hair off her face.

She slipped her arms about his neck, leaning in to kiss him. Her soft lips tempted him like no other, and the pit of his gut clenched. He could not lose her. He could not make a mistake and ruin what they had started to build between them.

But how to keep her happy? How to trust her? That he did not know, and the thought was alarming.

"Nor I, but then, you always seem to make it up to me when we do quarrel." She grinned, a wicked twist to her lips.

"Really?" he cooed. "And how do I do that?" he asked, even though he knew to what she was referring. They could both not get enough of each other at any given time.

Like right now. His cock hardened, and he hoisted her against him, wanting her to feel what she did to him.

Her eyes widened, and she bit her lip, tempting him even more. "You make me feel so good, Tatum. You give me such gratification," she answered, slipping off his lap to kneel before him. "But now I want to do the same for you." Her hand reached out, pushing against the fall of his breeches, her fingers tightening about his cock.

"You have tasted me, but I've yet to taste you. I know there must be a way. Please tell me what I can do. I need you." Her voice was like a Siren call he could not deny.

He swallowed, aching for her. "Take out my cock. We will start there," he said and groaned when she did as he asked, enthusiastically so.

EIGHTEEN

Millie stared a moment at Tatum's manhood that jutted before her face. He was large, long, his sex standing erect and taunting her to touch him.

Her fingers twitched to feel him, give him as much joy as he had given her. Show him with her touch, kisses, and intimacy how much he was starting to mean to her.

So much more than she ever thought possible, and she wanted to express that to him in any way she could.

"You can touch me," he said, leaning back and slipping one arm behind his head to watch her.

"With my hand or my mouth? Which one would you prefer?" she asked.

He closed his eyes, pain crossing his features. "Either. I want you to touch me with whatever you're comfortable with," he stated, his eyes darkening with need.

She understood that emotion well. She could not get enough of him either. Night and day, he was all she thought of now. How to reach his heart. How to win his love, make him faithful so he would never look at another woman again.

Make him forget his past that she knew to her very soul still haunted him and was between them, even now.

Millie reached out and stroked his phallus. It jerked against her palm, and she tightened her grip, stroking him from tip to base. The skin was soft, like velvet, and yet rigid too. She ached between her legs, wanting him there, filling and inflaming her.

All in good time, she promised herself. She teased for several minutes, changing her speed and strength while stroking him. A bead of pearl-colored liquid pooled at his tip, and she sliced her thumb over it, wanting to learn everything she could about her husband.

"That feels so good, Millie," he groaned when she increased her pace.

She smiled, wanting to do more than touch him. She licked her lips at the thought of placing him in her mouth. "Can I kiss you there?" she asked, unsure if that was what women did in this situation.

Tatum had kissed her sex and used his tongue

to make her reach such pleasurable heights that even now, she longed for him to do it again. But did that mean she could give Tatum a similar release?

"You can," he breathed. "You can suck it into your mouth. Use your tongue," he said, his breathing ragged.

Millie shuffled closer, bending over to place herself directly over his manhood. She licked the tip of his cock. Salty but pleasant. She covered his tip with her mouth, suckling the top of his cock before taking him farther down her throat. His size made it difficult to take him all in, but she did as much as possible.

He pushed into her mouth. His manhood, hard and demanding, stroked against her tongue. Using her hand, she teased the base of his manhood, stroking him as her mouth worked to bring him release.

His hands spiked into her hair, holding her against him, guiding her to ride his cock with her mouth.

She suckled him toward release, to spend in her mouth to give him everything a man and woman could have together, if only he would allow it.

"Enough," he gasped, pulling her from his manhood. He wrenched her onto his lap, and she straddled him, impaling herself without thought. Tremors shook her as he took her with relentless strokes, pushing and teasing her special place that begged for release.

She rode him, needing him to spend, to join her in ecstasy. He was an addiction, her husband, her love.

THE FIRST TREMORS OF HER RELEASE pounded between her legs, overflowing through her body, and she screamed his name, rocked atop him, and rode her release to its decadent end.

"Millie," he gasped, taking her lips in a searing kiss. "I cannot get enough of you," he declared, pumping his seed into her.

"Nor I, you," she admitted, kissing him back with all she felt for the man in her arms. She was supposed to make him fall in love with her, want her and no one else, but somehow the opposite had happened through her plan.

She had fallen in love with him.

Her husband. Her nemesis.

She loved him.

What would she do if he never loved her back?

THE FOLLOWING EVENING TATUM escorted Millie and Miss Smith to the theater, using the family box for the first time that Season. He nodded in welcome to those they met in the foyer before making their way upstairs.

He held the small of his wife's back. Her empire-cut, golden-embroidered silk gown made her appear regal and more beautiful than he had ever seen her before. The diamonds on her neck dipped low on her chest, pulling his gaze toward her bountiful breasts.

Hell, she was lovely. Made his chest ache.

He waited for the ladies to be seated before taking his own, watching Millie as she spoke with Miss Smith, her eagerness to watch the opera almost palpable.

He decided he liked pleasing her, making her happy.

When had that changed for him? When had he wanted to do nothing but spend time with her? Escort her to balls and parties. Make love to her all through the night.

Well, not always making love. His wife had an eagerness for fucking. A notion he was always willing to act upon. He wanted his mouth on her even now—the thought of tasting her here, an elixir like the sweetest wine.

He watched her, studied her profile, and his gut clenched. If hundreds of people did not surround them, he would kneel before her chair, bring her to release, and listen to her operatic melody.

"This is wonderful. Thank you for escorting

us, Your Grace," she said, reaching out to touch his hand.

Before she could pull away, he clasped her fingers, holding them in his lap.

Her smile brought warmth to his soul, her fingers playing with his as the *ton* took their seats for the night's entertainment. It wasn't long before the soprano began, yet he scarcely heard a note, not when a more distracting joy sat beside him.

Millie.

Her hand shifted on his lap and pushed against his falls. He glanced at her and noted the teasing smirk on her lips, all the while watching the stage with interest.

Tatum looked past Millie and saw that Miss Smith was paying no heed to them, completely engrossed in the vocalists on the stage.

His wife's fingers found his cock, and pushed down upon it, sliding along his length through his breeches. Need sliced through him, fast and hot, and his cock hardened.

She licked her lips, smiling now, and he shook his head. She was a minx who played with fire.

He leaned close. "Millie, what are you doing?" he whispered, pushing her hand harder against his manhood.

She faced him, biting her lip as if she were innocent of any accusation. She was not. She was as wicked as they came, and blast it, he loved that.

"I'm not doing anything, Your Grace. I'm merely enjoying the show," she said.

He shook his head. "Which show is that?" he asked, raising his brow.

She chuckled, her hand clasping him fully through his breeches and stroking him. He bit back a groan, glad of the dimmed lights in the theater, hopeful that no one could see what his duchess was doing to him.

Undoing him in front of them all without a care for the scandal she would cause if they were caught.

He stilled her wandering hand, pushing it to rest on his knee. "Behave, Duchess," he warned. The need to drag her from the box to one of the many abandoned rooms at the theater rioted through his blood.

"Do you not like my touch?" she asked him, pouting.

He breathed deep. Wanting to take her lip and nip it with his teeth. He swallowed, his hunger overriding his common sense. "You know that I do. More than I ever thought I would," he admitted. "I'm without shame, Duchess. I will have you if you keep taunting me so."

Her eyes flared at his warning, but her wicked touch told him she was anything but deterred.

Her hand slid playfully back up his leg, skimming past his cock but not touching it. "Very well," she sighed. "I shall behave."

Tatum shook his head, unable to school his features to one of indifference. He stood, taking his wife's hand and pulling her up beside him. "If you'll excuse us a moment, Miss Smith. Something has come up that I need to discuss with my wife."

Millie grinned at her friend, and Miss Smith's face blossomed as red as a rose before she nodded in understanding. "Of course. I shall wait here until your return."

Tatum all but dragged Millie from the box, striding down the hall, heedless to his wife trying to keep up with his steps. He looked into several rooms and, catching one with a desk, wrenched her inside, closing and locking the door behind him.

Millie strolled into the room, looking about and taking in the large desk, leather chair, and several bookcases that were scant of literature.

"What will you do to me in here, Your Grace? There was something you wanted to discuss with me, you said."

He growled, unable to stand another moment of her teasing. He knew what she was doing. He stalked toward her, pleased to see she understood his intent, and stepped back with every step forward he took.

He clasped her hips, smiling when her arse came up against the desk. She let out a little squeal of delight when he lifted her atop it, hoisting up her skirts to pool at her waist.

He licked two fingers and dipped them between her legs. So wet and ready. Her eyes widened, and she bit her lip, her eyes darkening with a hunger he understood well.

And it was just another thing to add to what he loved about her.

Nineteen

Her whole body yearned for the man before her. Would it always be like this between them? This madness over-powered her blood and made her do out-landish things, like being with him in chambers and homes that were not theirs.

When had they gone from bickering to be-deviled? He thrust into her, quick, hard pumps that drove deep. Sensation rippled over her skin, and she clung to him, seeking what only he could give her.

She wrapped her legs about his hips, holding him close, wanting him to make her reach the pinnacle of ecstasy he always achieved.

It did not take long.

He clasped her arse, angling her so with each stroke, he pushed her ever closer to release.

"Millie," he gasped, seizing her lips. "You're all

I want," he breathed, his tongue tangling with hers in a searing kiss.

Millie drank him in, reveling in his touch, his words. Her heart pounded, hopeful for their future. Did he love her and just couldn't say the words?

"Tatum," she moaned. The tremors of her release came quick and strong, and she gasped, holding him to enjoy every delicious drop of her release.

He spilled his seed in her, pumping and riding every last moment of their enjoyment to the end.

"What, my darling?" he asked when she did not continue her words.

Millie held his shoulders as he disengaged himself. He stepped back, his naughty smile making her lips twitch as he buttoned up the falls on his breeches.

Millie swallowed her nerves, no longer willing to live without stating her truth. A truth she hoped he, too, had come to realize was real.

"I'm in love with you, Tatum," she admitted, a weight lifting from her shoulders at saying how she felt. "Somehow, in our forced nuptials, angry outbursts, and passionate lovemaking, I've fallen in love with you," she said.

She wasn't sure what she expected from Tatum, but certainly not what came next. Tatum's face paled, and he moved back as if she were some strange object he did not know how to interpret.

He half-laughed, half-groaned, rubbing his hand over his jaw. "You are teasing me yet again, are you not?"

"Teasing you?" Millie said, shaking her head. "No, I'm perfectly sane and telling the truth. Even though you vexed me upon our first meeting and can be opinionated and wrong with those views, I've fallen in love with you somewhere in between our interactions. I love you," she said, not going to let him believe otherwise. There was no shame in admitting love.

"We have not been married two months. You cannot possibly be in love with me. As you say," he said, gesturing to her. "Our marriage was accomplished without either of us desiring the union. You cannot have fallen in love with me when I've been so disagreeable."

Millie slipped from the desk and adjusted her gown, ensuring nothing was out of place. She reached up, checking the pins in her hair, taking a moment to control the rioting emotions inside her heart.

Despair mostly.

What was he trying to say? What did he mean by such words? Did he still regret their marriage? Was he trying to say without words that he did not feel the same?

She pushed past him, needing to return to

the opera and ensure Paris was chaperoned. "We will discuss the matter when we're home. If you'll excuse me."

"Millie," he reached for her, pulling her back into the room. "I...I do not know how to respond to your honesty. I promised myself a long time ago that I would never allow myself to be hurt again, and I have kept that pledge. I do not think I'm capable of what you feel. Not with anyone."

Bile rose in Millie's throat, and she pulled from his grip. "Then I feel sad for you, Your Grace. For what is life without love? Excuse me," she said, leaving him in the abandoned room to return to their box.

Millie returned to her friend's side, who barely registered her arrival, so engrossed was she in the opera. She sat back down, schooling her features.

The singers on stage blurred, and she blinked, trying to stem the tears that threatened. Her husband did not love her. A truth she would need to reconcile with, considering they were married.

The hurt from her husband's rejection almost severed her in two. She placed her hands in her lap and swayed her mind into watching the story unfold on the stage that she was no longer interested in.

She was in love with a man who did not love her back.

However was she to survive a loveless marriage? How could she sit back and be indifferent when he took lovers or gained another mistress?

She could not.

She would live, laugh and be merry. She may never break her marriage vows, but she would enjoy her life. As much as she could in the situation in which she found herself.

That would have to be enough.

It will never be enough.

Tatum returned to the box at intermission, and a punch to the gut would have been less of a blow than the sight of Millie, animated with *joie de vivre* and laughing at something Lord Fox had said.

His lordship's interest in the duchess was evident, as was the sight of his lordship's hand low on Her Grace's back.

He would rip him limb from limb if his hand dipped any lower.

"What are you glowering at?" Howley said at his side, handing him a glass of brandy.

Tatum downed it. He knew he was staring at his wife, and he was aware other people in attendance had taken note.

He cared naught.

Anger rode hot and fast through his blood. Millie loved him, not Lord Fox. He had nothing to fear or question her over. She would not make a fool of him.

Surely she would not.

Would she?

"You look like a man about to commit murder," Howley mentioned, following his line of sight to the duchess. "Ah, I see what is bothering you." Howley chuckled. "Lord Fox may wish to bed your wife, but she will not break her vows."

"What makes you so sure?" Romney asked, losing sight of his lordship's hand when they moved to speak with their neighboring box, the Earl and Countess of Daniels.

"Because she's a Woodville, and those sisters are the fiercest, most loyal women I've ever met. Have you not seen your wife light up when you attend the same balls as her? When you dance with her?"

"No, I have not," he admitted. Was he blind to her delight by his insecurities? "When I arrive, she is usually in the arms of someone else."

"Women love to dance, Romney. That is all that is about," Howley said, watching him curiously. "Make an effort, Romney, or you may find yourself in a situation that even I could not foresee. Do not push everyone away as you always have. I made that mistake once, and it was only when I corrected that error that I was happy again."

Howley clapped him on the shoulder before

pulling back the curtain and leaving. Tatum ground his teeth. What was wrong with him that he still could not love? Could not trust?

He caught sight of Lady Sinclair. Eleanor was as handsome as she had always been, and he studied her, wondering why he allowed what she did to him to cloud his future.

To hurt his affinity with Millie.

Eleanor caught him staring, and she left the box she shared with several others, soon joining him at his side. He inwardly groaned, not wanting her to read into his interest with anything more than what it was. Merely trying to figure out his past to ensure his future did not meet the same fate.

"Romney," Eleanor said, dipping into a curtsy. She bussed his cheeks, and he stilled at her public display of affection.

He set her back from him, and she laughed, sidling up to him instead and entwining her arm with his. "You were staring at me, Your Grace. Is there somewhere you wish to go that you may be able to stare at me some more? I'm willing, you understand," she said, meeting his eye with salacious intent.

"I was not staring at you, Lady Sinclair, as a means to harness your attention. I was debating what it was that I ever saw in you. You are a flirt, a woman of no morals. I do not know why I thought you would ever be faithful to me when you could not be faithful toward the man you threw me over with."

She tsked tsked him, unperturbed by his words. Proving to him yet again what an unfeeling, unloving woman she was.

"Lord Sinclair was no more loyal to me than I was to him, and that suited us both. You were too in love with me, Romney. You thought I was the sun to your moon, the stars in your night sky, perfect and glittering always. But I did not want to be that kind of lady. While I want to be rich and have everything money can buy, I also wish for freedom. The marquess gave me that privilege. You would never have allowed me to be so unrestrained, and I would have suffocated under our marriage bed and made us both miserable."

Oddly, her words made sense, but they did not remove the hurt he had felt at the time. The shame. "You could have told me all of this before our wedding day. Prior to allowing me to believe I was going to be a father."

A look of shame crossed her features, the first he had ever seen on her before. "I apologize for doing that to you, truly. You deserved better, but you are happy now and have been happy since that day. Your mistress has been keeping your bed warm, and you have a wife who adores you. Why look at her now, watching us like a little lost kitten. Poor pet, she is wondering what we're talking about."

Tatum glanced across the box and saw Millie watching him. The hurt in her eyes tore pain through his chest before she turned, giving him her back. Damn it. He did not want her to see him talking to Eleanor. She would leap to conclusions that were not true.

Panic tore through when Eleanor's mocking laughter carried throughout the box. Along with the chastising glare Miss Smith bestowed upon him before following his wife's lead.

TWENTY

Millie left early the following evening for Lady Hirch's dinner party that she was to attend. Paris escorted her and had not brought up, thankfully, what had transpired the previous evening at the opera.

The carriage rolled to a halt before the small Georgian town house on St James's Square, and she ground her teeth at the thought of Tatum watching Eleanor like a pathetic fool.

They had just made passionate love. She had declared herself to him, bared her heart, and that was how he repaid such truth.

What was he thinking, even speaking to the woman who caused him so much pain? Unless he thought to make her his mistress...

After last evening, her attempts to make him see her, not just as the woman who accidentally forced marriage upon him, but as a woman he could love, were all in vain.

He did not love her. He would have stated he did if he held the slightest affection when she laid her heart out before him, baring herself to his ridicule and denial.

While he did not mock her statement, he certainly denied her his love. She would not try again. She would not hope that, in time, his feelings may become engaged. He had loved once and lost and seemed determined to keep his heart bottled away like some rare wine that no one could sample.

Millie took a calming breath and fought not to lose her composure. She would have to become cognizant that her marriage was an utter disaster, unlike all her sisters' unions.

Had started out terribly and had ended the same way.

Tears prickled, and she blinked, trying to halt them from slipping down her cheeks.

Without words, Paris clasped her hand, squeezing it. "People look at each other all the time at balls and parties, Millie. His Grace speaking to Lady Sinclair last evening may have been completely by chance, and you caught a second of his inspection. We do not know what that inspection may mean."

Millie shook her head, dabbing at her cheeks. "No. I watched him when he did not know I was looking. He could not take his eyes from her." She shook her head, not understanding why.

What was it that the woman held over him? They were engaged once, but was he so heartbroken that anyone who followed stood no chance of winning his heart?

Why would he allow her ladyship such power over him?

"Well, he can have Lady Sinclair and keep his former mistress for all I care. I will not be attending any more balls that he is attending. I do not want anything whatsoever to do with him."

"Should you not speak to the duke? He seemed distressed that you left after intermission instead of staying for the second act. I observed him before I followed you."

Millie shrugged, not caring how he felt. Not anymore. He did not care how she felt or that she loved him. He had not returned her regard, which was all she needed to know.

Bastard.

"Does the duke know you're attending Lady Hirch's dinner this evening?" Paris asked, pulling up her silk gloves as the carriage rocked to a halt before the town house.

"No. I left word with Thomas that I'm at the Maddigon's ball this evening. I will attend, of course, but not for several hours. The duke will not be there by the time we attend, and that is how I would prefer it."

Paris watched her, and she did not like the

pity she read in her friend's eyes or concern over her reaction to the duke.

A liveried footman opened the door, greeting them. They made their way indoors, the dinner guests congregating in the front parlor before dinner.

Lord Fox strolled over to her, taking her hand and kissing it in greeting. "Duchess," he said, his deep voice a welcome reprieve from her friends who only reminded her more of her disastrous evening with her husband. She did not want to think of the duke. Not tonight or ever again. He did not think of her, and she refused to dwell on him.

"How very fortunate of us to have you here this evening. You look very beautiful," he drawled, his gaze dipping to the neck of her gown.

Millie raised her chin, enjoying being the object of another's desire. Not that she would act upon such realizations, but it was a boost to one's confidence, and she so needed to be prized and flirted with a little right at this moment.

She cast him her best coquettish smile. "Why, thank you, Lord Fox. That is very kind of you to say," she said.

Paris excused herself, walking over to their hosts to speak to them, leaving Millie with his lordship.

"Not kind at all, Your Grace. I'm merely

pointing out a matter of fact." He came and stood beside her, waving over a footman for a glass of wine. He handed her a flute, tipping his glass against hers. "I will admit I'm pleased you're alone this evening, other than with your dearest friend. It will mean I can monopolize your time."

Millie chuckled, assessing Lord Fox. He was tall, muscular, and had a jawline that Adonis would have been jealous of. The type of gentleman she would have welcomed to court her had she been given a choice to have a Season as she wished.

Right at this moment, she could have been courted by this man for several weeks. Maybe he would have fallen in love with her. Not that he would now. Not that anyone would, it seemed. She was doomed to live a loveless life where she pined for something she would never gain.

Millie took a long sip of her wine, dulling the pain such a thought darted through her. "You will only be able to do so should you sit beside me at dinner, my lord."

"Oh, do not worry about that, Your Grace. I have spoken to Lady Hirch, and she has placed me beside you as I wished."

Millie met his blue eyes and read the wickedness burning bright. "Really?" She laughed. "Are you so eager as that to sit beside me? I wonder why," she said, enjoying his company and teasing.

"Can you not guess my ultimate plan,

Duchess?" He grinned, biting his lip in a way that made her catch her breath.

"No," she answered, clearing her throat and taking a calming breath herself.

"You're an intelligent, beautiful woman. I will leave you to ponder that answer and ask you again in a week or two if you're any wiser to my goal," he said. The dinner gong sounded loud somewhere in the house, and he held out his arm. "Shall we?" he asked her.

Millie slipped her arm through his, letting him lead her from the room. She had not expected to enjoy tonight's dinner or ball, but with Lord Fox more than willing to keep her mind from pondering her husband, well, what was there not to like?

TATUM SEARCHED THE MADDIGON'S BALL and could not see Millie or Miss Smith anywhere. He checked the supper room, the terrace, and may have lingered about the retiring room for a time, but to no avail.

She was not here.

He spied her sister Lady Leigh and made his way over to her, bowing and bussing her cheeks in welcome.

"Your Grace," she said, smiling at him. Lady Leigh's smile reminded Tatum of his wife and increased his need to find her. "How are you this evening? Is the duchess with you?" she asked him, looking past him as if to find his wife.

He shook his head, his search for his wife continuing as he stood beside Lady Leigh. "She is not. I thought she was to attend this ball, and I was to meet her here. But I may have been wrong," he said, frowning.

Lady Leigh's brow furrowed, and his concern doubled. He fought not to ask outright where Millie could be, but he could not. People already spoke of their marriage enough. He did not need any more rumors to become attached to it.

"I'm sure she will be here soon," Lady Leigh said, laying a consoling hand on his arm.

The pit of his stomach clenched, and as much as he wanted to think that Millie would be here soon, something told him she would not be. She was angry with him, had locked him out of her room last evening, and was out with Miss Smith before he came downstairs to breakfast.

Her anger at him was all his fault. He had caused her pain, and now she was avoiding him.

Where was she?

Tatum remained at the ball for several more hours, and still, his wife did not arrive. He glanced about the ballroom, sipping his brandy, having lost count of how many he'd had. People glanced in his direction, watching him, turning back to their friends and whispering words he could not hear.

Were they laughing at him? Did they speak of his being here and his wife's absence? Of course they did. The *ton* loved a good scandal, and it would not be a shock to any of them that he would give them another beauty.

He downed his drink and strode from the ballroom. Maybe Millie had returned home and had changed her mind about the Maddigon's ball. He remembered his butler's statement of his wife's movements for the evening. Perhaps his aging butler had become confused and muddled with her plans.

He arrived home and strode up to their suite of rooms. Not bothering to knock on her door, he strode into her space and felt the blood drain from his face.

Her maid sat before a small fire, mending a shift of Millie's, it seemed, but as for his wife, there was no sign.

The maid stood and dipped into a curtsy. "Your Grace, good evening," she said.

He nodded, annoyance replacing a little of his concern. "Notify me when the duchess returns home. Thank you," he barked and left, striding to the library.

He poured himself a brandy and several more and studied the fire as it slowly burned to nothing but coals.

His wife's maid never notified him of his wife's return, and nor did she arrive home.

TWENTY-ONE

Over the next week, Millie avoided her husband at the numerous events she attended. At home was another matter altogether, and she found it increasingly difficult to remain away from him. Especially when he sought her out often. Not that she wasn't prepared for such situations. She had discussed the matter with Paris, and even though her friend thought it best that she speak to the duke, Millie refused to relent. She had planned to leave the moment he tried talking to her, which had worked, up to today at least.

He had not returned her feelings and had left her looking like a lovesick fool. Therefore, she would do as she liked for the remainder of the Season and couldn't care less what the duke had to say about it.

Thankfully, however, several days into her

giving the duke the cut direct, he had seemingly given up trying to speak to her or attend events that she did. Proving her point yet again that he did not care at all. She was nothing to him but a wife who warmed his bed, and even that had ceased.

He likely had his mistress bought and booked since he stopped shadowing her bedroom door. Last week at the opera, he probably discussed the arrangement with Lady Sinclair right under her nose.

The thought made her stomach riot, and she took a calming breath, determined to enjoy a night at Vauxhall's Pleasure Gardens. She had arrived with her sister Hailey and several of the duchess's friends. Her friends now too, she supposed.

Paris linked arms with her as they made their way to their private supper boxes. The music and dancing were already ongoing. People flocked everywhere, lanterns and flowers decorating the outdoor ball.

"What a shame the duke is not to attend this evening," Paris said, giving her a pointed stare. "You do need to speak to him, Millie. He does not look happy, and neither do you."

Millie huffed, having not one notion of relenting to him. If he wanted to make amends, apologize and offer his love, then and only then would it be worth her effort to listen to him. If not, she was in no better situation than she now found herself. Not that her friend seemed to listen to her reasoning, and she was sick of trying to make her understand her point of view.

"Let us not talk of the duke. There are more enjoyable times to be had than thinking and speaking of a man who does not care what I do."

"I do doubt that," Paris said. "Have you not seen him look at you? He looks positively despondent."

"I'm sure Lady Sinclair will pull him out of his melancholy," she tartly returned, smiling at Lord Fox, who was awaiting them at their box. He waved for her to join him where he sat.

Paris clasped Millie's arm, halting her steps. "There is no future with Lord Fox. Please remember that before you do anything foolish."

Millie let go of her friend's arm. "I may enjoy the company of others, but I will not break my vow. I promise you," she said, joining his lordship. He stood upon her arrival, taking her hand and bussing her silk gloves with a kiss.

"Good evening, Duchess. I hope you're prepared to dance this evening?"

She smiled and took her seat. "I'm more than ready." Millie watched the *ton* at play before their box. They were to dine first and then attend the ball, and already the scent of beef and vegetables floated in the night air.

"The duke has left you alone once again. His absence is my gain."

If Lord Fox's words were not proof enough of his growing attraction toward her, the look he bestowed certainly left Millie with little doubt of his intentions.

She did not want to do anything with the earl, but nor did she want his flirtation to end. It was pleasant to be wanted, to be courted and not forced into something she did not want. Romney had not tried anything of the kind. The thought left her dejected, and she fought to keep the smile on her face.

"You flatter me, my lord," she said.

"And he is wrong," a deep, aggravated tone stated from behind.

Millie stilled hearing Romney's words that held a voiceless warning. How long had he been standing behind them? Listening to everything that was being said?

Lord Fox stood, his bow short and quick. "Romney, good of you to join us. Please be seated."

Romney came up to the table and, without a by-your-leave, sat in Lord Fox's seat.

Millie could not meet his eyes, although the burning gaze upon her cheek left heat to kiss her skin.

"Duchess," he said, his tone putting her on alert.

"Duke," she answered, sipping her wine. "I did not think you were attending this evening."

He laughed, but the sound held no amusement. "More like you thought I did not know where you were going and did not think I would figure it out. But alas, you see, the Vauxhall outdoor ball is an event few would miss, and your sister invited me to the supper box."

Millie turned and found Hailey watching her keenly. Her sister gave her a small smile before turning back to speak to her guests.

What a traitor her sister was. She would have words with her when they were alone next.

Millie spied Lady Sinclair move past their box, and the devil sat on her shoulder, wanting to hurt the man at her side as much as he hurt her. "Oh, look there," she said to Romney. "Lady Sinclair is present. Your attendance here now becomes utterly transparent."

"Come with me. Now," Romney demanded, standing and pulling her up to go with him.

Not wanting to make a scene, she proceeded with him into the gardens, Romney taking her down a dim walk and stopping at the base of the Triumphal Arches. She walked ahead of him, fire licking at her wounded heart.

"What are you about, Millie? Attending events that I know not of. Being here, seated next to Lord Fox as if he is the one you married and not me. What are you doing?"

Millie gaped and closed her mouth with a snap. What was she doing? Had the man lost control of his senses? "I'm attending balls and dinners as is my right as a duchess. I have been invited, and therefore I shall attend. That you do not know my social calendar is not my issue, Your Grace."

He set his hands on his hips, staring at her as if she had lost her mind. She had done nothing of the sort. She may have had once when she told him she loved him, but once again, she was in charge of her senses.

"I do know where you're supposed to attend, but when I go to meet you there, you're never present. I know you're avoiding me. You lock the door between our chambers, and we rarely cross paths in the house anymore. What is going on, Millie? What are you doing that you do not want me to know about?"

His words added fuel to her anger, and she understood perfectly what he was saying. "You accuse me of acting inappropriately when I catch you, not five minutes after declaring myself to you watching your delightful Lady Sinclair. Pining over her like some lovesick popinjay."

"What?" he gasped. "I am not pining over anyone," he declared.

"You think that I'm blind? Well, Your Grace, I am not. I know you still care for her ladyship. That you never got over her choice."

He cringed, shaking his head in denial. "On the day of the wedding, she sent a note by her lady's maid to the church informing me she had married Lord Sinclair and that our understanding was at an end. But that was eight years ago. I can assure you I harbor no affections toward a woman who could do such a thing to me or anyone."

"And yet you speak to her still? Dance with her, perhaps? Are you not the one who is mad and up to something you should not be?" she said, stepping closer to him, needing to see him clearer in the darkened gardens. "It is obvious to me and anyone who sees you with her that you're still in love with her ladyship."

"I am not in love with her anymore."

His words did not soothe Millie's hurt. If anything, hearing him declare he once was in love with her ladyship hurt even more. He had never stated so to her. Had flatly refused to say anything at all when she stood before him telling him her truth.

"Do not lie to me, Tatum, and certainly do not lie to yourself. We made a mistake, and our marriage should never have happened. You are in love with a woman who is not your wife, and as much as I want to fault you for that, I cannot. The affections you built with Lady Sinclair came long before me. Our marriage was foolish and a mistake. My declaration of love was also wrong. I should not have said what I did, and I apologize for adding further burdens to your life."

"Millie," he said, reaching out and trying to pull her toward him.

She stepped out of his reach, not wanting him to touch her. "Do not feel as though you have to say anything to me. We are married, nothing can change that fact, but I was confused. My desire clouded my judgment, and I said things I should not."

"What are you trying to say? You want to live separate lives?" Confusion clouded his handsome face. Millie stopped herself from reaching out, to hold him, force him to care for her. She would not beg like some wretched woman with no morals. She would not degrade herself further. If he touched her again, she would be lost, and she would not give him that power.

"I think it is best that we do. You may have your mistress, whomever you want that to be, and I shall live under the protection of your name."

A muscle worked in his jaw at her words, and he glowered at her across the dark pathway.

"You will take a lover?"

The words were like a blow to her heart. "No, I will not. But I will not stop you from doing so. You may do whatever the hell you like." Millie swept past him, leaving him to gape at her.

She did not return to the box but instead

walked to where her driver and footman stood and requested to be returned home. She would send a note to Paris to return home without her later. Her friend would understand.

If only Millie's heart would as well.

TWENTY-TWO

Tatum watched Millie walk back toward the Vauxhall ball, her back defiantly straight, her head held high, even though he knew she was hurt. That she was lying.

She had to be. No one fell out of love with someone in a week. He knew that better than most. But she was wrong. He no longer loved Lady Sinclair. In fact, he debated if he liked her at all, which thinking upon the matter, he did not.

He returned to the supper box and found Millie absent, and his heart sank. Had she returned home? Was she so upset that she no longer wanted to attend this ball that was one of the Season's highlights?

"Is the duchess not with you, Your Grace?" Miss Smith asked him, looking about the guests, trying to place Millie.

Tatum cleared his throat, shaking his head.

"Ah, no, she is not. I think she has returned home," he said.

"And should you not do the same?" Miss Smith asked him, the warning in her words easy to hear.

"I do not think she wants me at home or anywhere near her right at this moment," he said truthfully, rubbing a hand over his jaw.

Miss Smith scoffed, sipping her wine. "Are all men blind? I thought you had more sense than others, but maybe I was giving you more credit than you're due."

"I beg your pardon?" he said, affronted. Never in his life had some miss from anywhere ever spoken to him so. Well, that wasn't necessarily true. Millie had certainly told him her opinions before they were married, and she too was from Grafton.

What kind of ladies did they breed in that village?

"I think you ought to return home and ensure the duchess is safe. I shall have the Duchess of Derby chaperone me for the evening," she said, her unnerving stare making him question himself.

Tatum glanced about the box and noted that Lord Fox was nowhere to be seen. An uncomfortable knot lodged in his gut, and he nodded. "Very well. I shall go," he said, leaving and not bothering to address anyone on his way out.

Tatum hailed a hackney and returned home posthaste, wanting to speak to Millie further and mend the damage his silence had caused. He strode into the foyer, determined to make things right, and his steps faltered at the sight of Lord Fox standing before his wife, wiping tears from her cheeks.

Rage tore through him at the sight of his wife all but in the arms of another man. In his home before his staff. Reminiscent of another time when his then betrothed left him standing before all the *ton*, only to send a note telling him she would not arrive.

"Get your hands off my wife." His tone brooked no argument, and Lord Fox stepped back, sensing his anger, and rightfully so.

"I escorted the duchess home. Nothing more, Romney," Lord Fox stated, holding up his hands, trying to appease him.

Tatum would not hear a word of it. All he could see was his wife in another man's arms. Or at least all but wrapped up in his hold. Did the bastard think to make Millie his lover? Over his corpse, would he ever allow anyone to touch his wife.

He lunged and tackled Lord Fox to the marble floor. His lordship attempted to drive him off, but Tatum would not relent. He got in two good knuckle hits to the bastard's jaw and nose before he received one in return.

Blood filled his mouth, and he welcomed the metallic taste, if only to give him more reason to pummel the bastard to a pulp.

The sound of Millie yelling for him to stop, for them both to stop, sounded behind him. But he would not. The bastard would pay for trying to make his wife his mistress. Maybe she was already.

The thought brought another fist to the bastard's face, opening up a cut above his eye.

"Enough, Your Grace," his butler shouted.

Hands wrapped about his arms, pulling him up and off Lord Fox, who lay on the floor, bloodied and disheveled.

Tatum tried to reach for the bastard again but to no avail. His footmen had him firmly held.

"Go, Lord Fox. Thank you for escorting me home, and I am dreadfully sorry for my husband's outburst," Millie said, sending him a scolding look.

She tried to help his lordship stand, and anger ripped through him a second time. Never had he ever wanted to rip another man's limbs from his body.

"Do not touch him, Millie." He hated that her slightest assistance left him vulnerable.

Lord Fox stumbled to his feet and strode from the room without another word, leaving them. Tatum shook free of his servant's hold, dismissing them. "Library, now, Duchess," he barked, not waiting for her to follow him into the room.

She did as he asked, shutting the door and rounding on him. "What do you think you're doing? People will talk about what just happened, making me look guilty for something I am not."

"Are you not guilty of it?" he accused. He fisted his hands at his sides to stop their shaking. "You looked more than comfortable in his embrace just a moment before."

"And you looked more than comfortable staring forlornly at Lady Sinclair." She strolled up to him, staring down her nose at him. Not something he thought possible due to her height, but there it was. "You're incapable of love and never wished to marry me. I know that more than anyone since you could not return the feelings I admitted to you. But do not think me a fool not to know why that is so. You're still in love with Lady Sinclair, and there is nothing I can do to change that fact," she said, clasping her brow in thought. "But do not think I will not allow myself to enjoy what little happiness this marriage will afford me. Men may say pretty things to me, dance, and want more from me, but I'm not you, Duke. I will not break my vows, even though I know you fully intended to do that to me when we married."

Tatum ran a hand through his hair, his stomach in knots. She was so withdrawn from him. It was as if she had given up on him, on what she felt for him. Saw him as worthless.

"I'm not in love with Lady Sinclair, and I care for you. More than I thought I would care for anyone ever again. I do not want our marriage to be like this, Millie."

"You care for me but do not love me. I cannot take back what happened to you, Tatum. I cannot change the past. Only you can change how we go on in the future."

He reached out, taking her hands. She moved out of his hold and walked to the mantel to stare at the small fire.

"Can I trust you, Millie? Your actions this evening tell me I cannot."

He cringed at the hurt that crossed her features. He did not want to harm her. Damn it all to hell. He wanted to trust her, love her as she deserved. But nor could he survive another heartbreak. To lose Millie as he lost Lady Sinclair would hurt far worse and would be something from which he would never recover.

"The real question is, can I trust *you*, Tatum?" She met his eyes, and he swallowed hard at the tears that sat on the brink of falling. "I do not think I can," she said, leaving him alone once again.

TWENTY-THREE

Millie curled up in bed the following morning, her heart sore and her stomach cramping, making her dizzy. She stared out the windows, watching a few wispy clouds in the sky, and listened to her maid bustle about in the room, preparing her for the day.

Not that she felt like doing anything at all. If she never went anywhere ever again, it would be too soon. She wasn't fooled enough not to know that their servants had probably already talked of her husband's fisticuffs last evening with Lord Fox with other servants in town. Perhaps there was already a rumor that she was having an illicit affair of some kind, making her husband look the fool again, but with his wife this time. Not his betrothed.

The thought made bile rise in her throat, and she lunged from the bed, seeking out her washing bowl before emptying her stomach contents into it.

"Oh, Your Grace," her maid cried, coming to her aid, pulling back her hair, and patting her forehead with a damp cloth. "What is the matter? Do you think it was your tea this morning?" she asked.

Millie shook her head. "No, I'm certain that was perfectly fine. I'm just feeling unwell all of a sudden." She took a deep breath, which did little to soothe her upset tummy. "A glass of water, please, Eve," she said, allowing her maid to help her stand and escort her back to bed.

She huddled under the blankets, only sat up a little to have a small sip of water before lying back down.

"Let us hope that it is only of short duration, Your Grace," Eve said, watching her keenly.

Millie nodded. "I'm certain it will be."

THE SICKNESS DID NOT ABATE. IN FACT, several days later, Millie could not help but wonder if her upset stomach was not merely nerves but something precious and wanted. On her behalf in any case.

Most afternoons, she felt well again and could attend most balls and parties, even if her gowns, especially the bodice area, had become a little uncomfortable to wear.

Not that she enjoyed society much of late. It seemed the rumors had taken hold regarding what happened between the duke and Lord Fox. That both gentlemen were sporting cut faces and bruised cheeks did not help the matter.

Worse was, she now had to tell Tatum that she was pregnant. Would he believe the child was his? The thought of him or the *ton* thinking it was Lord Fox's simply because he escorted her home was a humiliation she could not bear.

She was not the type of woman who played men the fools. Unlike Lady Sinclair, who seemed to do it with ease and little shame, or at least she had before marrying the marquess over the duke.

"A bath, please, Eve," she requested, sipping her tea before the fire while waiting for the servants to fill up her tub. If she were having a baby, a future lady, or a duke, then she needed her rest. She would have to stop worrying about what the *ton* believed or what Romney was up to. If a baby was coming, that was her priority now.

Millie sank under the water in the bath, rinsing her hair. She came back up and heard her maid at the door, speaking to someone before it closed again, and silence ensued.

"Eve would you pass me the soap, please," she said.

Instead of her maid, Tatum walked into her bathing room, stopping at the threshold to lean against the wall. "I've been informed that you're unwell. What is the matter?" he asked, watching her.

"Please hand me the soap," she asked, stalling.

He moved farther into the room, picking up the bar that smelled of jasmine and handing it to her.

She took it without a word and played with the soap in her hands, not bothering to cover herself from his view. After all, he was her husband and should know what he had lost due to his continued infatuation with Lady Sinclair.

His eyes dipped to her chest, and goosebumps rose on her skin. Knowing there was no use in lying to him as he would find out eventually, she decided to tell him the truth. "If you must know, I believe I'm having a baby. The doctor is due here today to confirm," she said, matter-of-fact. One time she had hoped that such words would have been a blessing, a time for celebration and joy for them both. And although she felt all those things, she did not think Tatum did. She was not his love. Why would he want anything from her, including a child?

His eyes widened before he blurted, "You're pregnant?" he stated. "Is it..."

Millie stood, fully aware of what he was about to say. She flung the soap at him, pleased when it whacked him in the forehead. "Do not dare finish that question, Tatum, or I shall leave you and bedamned the scandal that comes of it.

And damn you along with it," she said, stepping out of the bath.

Her foot slipped on the floorboards, and she reached out to clutch the bath but missed the edge. Tatum's hands wrapped around her waist, halting her fall, and she took a calming breath, her heart pumping loud in her ears.

He set her on her feet, passing her a linen towel. "Thank you," she said, wrapping it around her.

He stared at her, and she swallowed the lump in her throat. Something she could not fathom flickered in his dark-blue eyes before he blinked, and it was gone. "Millie, please forgive me. I'm sorry. Sorry for everything I have made you feel and what you have seen. I never intended to hurt you," he said. "You must know that is true."

She pushed past him, going over to where her maid had left her shift and stockings. "I do not want to talk about us anymore. That subject is long over. I have a child to think about now. The baby will receive all the love I have to bestow, and that will be enough."

TATUM CURSED HIMSELF THE BIGGEST, stupidest fool who lived in England. How could he have allowed his wife to believe what she said was true? It was as far from the truth as could be.

"Millie, that is not enough for me. I do not

want you to only live for your children. I want you to live for us as well."

"That is unlikely," she taunted, slipping the shift over her head and removing the delicious view of her arse.

He breathed deep, fighting the urge to seduce her to his will. That would not work today. Today he needed to keep his senses intact so she would believe him when he did tell her all that he felt for her.

"I'm in love with you," he said, reaching for her hands and forcing her to allow him to hold them, even when she tried to pull away.

She stared at him, her eyes wary. "I do not believe you."

She shouldn't believe him. Hell, after everything he had put her through, it would be hard to think he ever spoke the truth. But he did love her and needed her to believe him.

"I know I have muddled things between us. I pushed you away and ran scared when you told me how you felt. I should not have done that, and I'm sorry, Millie."

She watched him, and he wished he could know what she was thinking. How she felt about him now. Could he win her heart back after he made her believe she did not warrant the emotion from him?

"What has changed?" she asked him. "The baby? Is that why you're professing your love to me now? Because if that is the only reason why I do not want it." She pulled away and strode into her room, picking up her shawl and wrapping it about her shoulders.

She sat on the edge of her bed, her hand comforting her stomach and the life that grew there.

He kneeled before her, willing to beg if he had to. "I was so blinded by my pride that I swore a long time ago, long before meeting you, that I would never make myself as vulnerable as I had with Lady Sinclair." He clasped Millie's hands, needing to touch her. "We were intimate, Millie, and she said she was pregnant as a way to bring our marriage forward. I thought myself in love with her and was more than pleased to follow her lead. But what I did not know was Lord Sinclair, a gentleman far older than I or Eleanor, was also far richer. He was a marquess and I merely a lord at that time, but he had not offered marriage, even when Eleanor told him she was *enceinte*. She panicked, I suppose," he said, unable to blame Eleanor totally for her duplicity.

"She was desperate to save herself and give the baby legitimacy, and so she hurled herself at me one night at a ball and then informed me not a month later that I was to be a father. I was ecstatic, of course, but naïve. When Lord Sinclair heard of our betrothal, he took steps to ensure she returned to his side and eventually did the right thing by her, and they married. But I was left heartbroken, a young man of eighteen who was introduced to love and lies in the worst way imaginable, and I punished anyone from that day forward who wanted to get close to me. You included."

Millie did not say anything, merely watched him, debated his words. Would she believe his truth, as sad and honest as it was?

"And now you're ready to love again. To love me, you say?" she stated, her cynical tone making his gut churn.

"I am," he said. "Please believe me that I am."

Twenty-Four

The words spilling from Tatum's lips were words she had long dreamed of hearing. She had cried and despaired over, yet still wondered if he were being truthful.

"I have never once been unfaithful to you. Granted, our marriage did not have a conventional beginning, but the more time I spent in your company, learned of you and your life, your family, when we were intimate, I could not help but love you for all that you are. To have my declaration ignored is not something one can merely overcome and forget."

"I understand." He came and sat beside her. "I did not want to believe that you loved me, for then I would have to face what I've known for several weeks. That no matter my struggles to ignore what was happening between us, I could no longer continue. I loved you long before you told me how you felt, but I was too stupid and pig-headed, too obstinate to admit that to myself."

Hope began to seep into her heart at his words. "You accused me of being unfaithful. Have been terribly jealous at balls and parties. If you love me as you say, that must change. I will not partake in balls and parties if you're glowering and then chastising me later over my conduct. I wanted a marriage of love and affection, of trust, as my sisters have all been fortunate to secure. When we married, I thought any hope of such a future was gone, but I was wrong. I also will not be accused of breaking my vows. I'm not the one who had a mistress or a previous betrothed in this marriage. If anyone between us," she said, gesturing to them both, "should have complications in trusting, it ought to be me."

He cringed at her words, and she was glad of it. He needed to hear all her thoughts, whether they were sweet or not.

"I was jealous, Millie. So jealous of anyone who glanced your way that I could not restrain myself. I watched the men admire you, want to dance and flirt, and it clouded my judgment. I knew you had wanted a Season. You begged your parents on the day we were caught to believe you so you could take your curtsy before the queen and find a great love match, but do you not see?" he said, clasping her cheeks in his hands. "Do you not know that you have found what you sought?

I'm your grand love match. I have my faults, I do not deny it, but I will fight to keep you as you're the most wonderful woman I've ever met.

"Looking back, I know now that I never loved Lady Sinclair. That was a youth's foolish folly. What I feel for you, Millie is so much more. My heart stops at the very sight of you. I smile each time I hear your voice somewhere in the house. Your laughter makes me laugh, even if I do not know what it is that you've found amusing. You are wickedly fun and flirtatious, not to mention passionate. I do not want to lose you, and certainly not because I was too scared to give my heart a second chance. I know you will keep my heart safe as I will keep yours. Please do not pull away from me. I made a mistake. I will not make another. I promise you."

Millie swallowed the lump in her throat at Tatum's words. She sniffed, blinking at the tears that blurred her vision. "The baby is yours, Tatum. I would never be unfaithful to you, even if I were angry at you," she said.

He pulled her into his arms, holding her tight. "I know, love. I'm a fool and should never have questioned you."

She took a calming breath, the scent of sandalwood teasing her senses. Oh, how she had missed him while they were apart. She wrapped her arms about him, holding him close. "I should never have pushed you to think I would seek comfort elsewhere. That was wrong, and I would never act on anything you may have envisioned. I wanted to make you jealous and see what you would lose if you did not admit the truth to yourself."

He chuckled, pulling back to meet her eyes. "Did you suspect that I was in love with you all the time and just unable to admit it to myself?"

She nodded. "Yes, that was what I hoped, and it seems my wishes have come true." She grinned, clasping his jaw before sliding her hands into his hair. His locks tumbled through her fingers, and she linked her hands at his nape.

"Watching you dance with anyone, Lord Fox especially, made me forget who I was and what was expected of me. I should not have lashed out at his lordship, and I will apologize to him for my actions. But to think of you seeking love elsewhere when I was too foolish to admit my feelings was torture more painful than anything I have ever endured. You, Millie Woodville, now the Duchess of Romney, are my true love. My first and last love on this earth, and I adore you. Please say you forgive me," he said.

Millie was nodding before he finished his plea. "I forgive you, you vexing man, and I love you too," she said, her heart full of hope and love. So much love.

He kissed her then, swept her onto his lap, and devoured her mouth. All the joy, the expectation of what they were about to embark on was in the kiss.

Passion, love, adoration. Everything she had ever wanted in a marriage, in a husband, she had gained. All that she dreamed. Her match in every way.

Tatum stood and lay her on the bed, coming down beside her. He wiggled his brows before pushing her shawl off her shoulders and removing the shift she wore.

Goosebumps rose on her skin when his eyes darkened with hunger. A need that she too felt and had longed for since their estrangement.

"So beautiful and mine," he whispered, his finger tracing her collarbone with exquisite care before dipping between her breasts, paying homage to both her nipples and leaving them puckered and hard.

Millie squirmed under his touch, and an ache thrummed between her legs. "I want you so much, Tatum," she admitted, praying that his hand would dip farther still and touch her where she hungered.

His lips teased the underside of her ear, sending shivers down her spine. She reached for him, needing him, and he did not deny her. He moved over her, settling between her legs. Millie hooked her legs over his hips, her body alive with anticipation and need.

"Please, stop teasing me," she begged, reaching down to untie his front falls.

His manhood pushed into her hand, and she stroked him. So soft yet hard. Tatum groaned, and she reveled in his desire.

"That feels so good, Millie," he breathed against her lips, kissing her softly. "I'm going to make you feel good too," he promised her.

She pushed down his breeches, unable to wait a minute longer. Tatum thrust into her in one smooth stroke, filling and inflaming her more than she ever thought possible.

"Yes," she gasped, rocking against him. "I have missed this. I have missed you," she said, their eyes clashing.

He kissed her deep and long, his tongue tangling with hers as he took her with relentless strokes. "I have missed you too," he said. "Never draw from me again. I could not bear it."

She slipped her arms about his shoulders, the corded muscles in his back flexing with every stroke. "I promise I will never do so again."

Millie lost herself to him, letting herself enjoy and revel in all he did to her. What he made her feel. He filled and teased the special spot deep in her womb. Tremors and exquisite pleasure rocked through her, and she came apart in his arms. Spasm after delicious spasm shot to every part of her body.

"I love making you come," he admitted, his release following hers.

Millie treasured it too. Never would she ever tire of having him, of loving him as she did. "I will never hurt you again, my darling. I will love you to my dying day."

Tatum flopped beside her, and Millie stretched over him, not ready to end this exquisite interlude. She idly played with his chiseled chest, both catching their breaths. "Do you know, I believe that is one point in our marriage that we agree wholeheartedly upon."

He leaned down and kissed her nose, smiling. "It was bound to happen sometime that I do not vex you so much that we argue."

She laughed. "That is true." She leaned up to steal another kiss. A kiss that was merely the start of many more to come.

EPILOGUE

Millie was certain that if she grew any larger, she would not fit through the doorways of their home. She lay in the library, listening to her husband discussing estate business with his steward Mr. East elsewhere in the room while trying to elevate her feet since she had lost sight of her ankles several weeks ago.

She rubbed her belly, not immune to the continual ache that repeated itself every few minutes but never grew any worse. Tatum had sent for their London doctor a month ago, and he would be a guest at the estate until after the birth.

Millie grinned. Her husband was a worrier and expert planner, but she could not complain. He had taken care of her these past months better than any other time in her life, and she was a very contented wife.

A finger ran down her cheek before her seat dipped. "How are you feeling, my love? You've been quiet today," he said.

Millie opened her eyes, reveling in the sight of her handsome duke. She sighed, content beyond words that their marriage was happy. "I'm well, darling. A little uncomfortable, but nothing to alarm you with," she said, giving him her hand. "Please help me to stand. I think I shall return to my room and request a bath. They always make me feel a little better."

Tatum took her hand and did as she asked. He picked up her legs, swung them over the edge of the settee, and pulled her to her feet.

No sooner had he done so than a rush of water released between her legs. Millie gasped, staring at the puddle of water on the Aubusson rug. Tatum's shocked visage met hers an instant later.

"What was that?" He grabbed her. "Darling, are you well?" he asked.

Pain rocketed through her, and she doubled over, clutching her stomach. "I think...I think the baby is coming," she gasped, the room spinning, her breath catching as the pain contracted on her stomach and tightened to an unbearable amount.

"Mr. East, ring for a servant," her husband barked. "Now, man."

The pain lessened a minute or so later, and she stood straight, feeling well again. "Do not worry, Tatum. I feel like myself again now," she said before the pain increased a second time.

She let out a little yelp as the butler strolled into the room. "Your Graces?" he asked. "You called."

"Doctor, Thomas. Now!"

Millie caught sight of the butler's startled visage in the mirror above the mantel before he raced from the room, the door hitting the wall in haste.

"Do you think you can walk to your room, Millie?" Tatum asked her.

She shook her head, breathing deep and fighting the urge to push. "No, no, no, no, no, no, no, I cannot. Please give me a moment," she gasped, wincing in pain.

Millie heard the doctor barking orders before he strolled into the room, coming over to them. "Now, Your Grace, I think it is time," he said, reaching out to feel her stomach. "Ah, very good. I can feel you're contracting nicely." He stood back, meeting the duke's eye. "When this contraction decreases, we'll move the duchess upstairs. She will be more comfortable there."

Millie nodded and fought to breathe and not panic. The pain was atrocious. However did Hailey survive such a trauma? How did any woman?

"I feel a little better again," she said when her stomach stopped feeling like it wanted to rip in two.

Tatum did not bother assisting her. Instead, he hoisted her into his arms, no small feat considering she weighed the same as a young elephant at present.

"Tatum put me down. You'll drop me and hurt the baby," she demanded.

He ignored her, carrying her as if she weighed no more than a leaf. "I will never hurt you, my darling. But nor will I permit you to suffer on your way to our room," he said.

She allowed him his way, mostly because a third contraction came upon her with such ferocity that she was glad she was in his arms. She winced, fought for breath, and tried to breathe through the pain. Nothing worked, not her breathing, not clasping her stomach.

Nothing.

Oh dear God, this was awful.

Women must be bottle-headed to want children, especially if it was this painful to push them out.

She did not even want to think about that.

TATUM MANAGED TO CARRY MILLIE TO their room. No small exertion. She was nine months pregnant, after all. Not that he did not adore her as she was, but carrying a woman with a large frontward bulge was not the easiest thing to attempt.

He placed her on the bed, taking a calming breath when she sank into the cushions and linen, sighing in relief.

"The contraction is calming again," she said, running a hand over her stomach. Her eyes met his, and he caught the moment they widened again with renewed pain.

"It's back. I'm not ready," she stated, reaching for him. "It hurts, Tatum." Tears pooled in her eyes before she winced and fought through this next wave of pain.

"Doctor, what is happening?" Tatum asked.

The doctor ordered the staff who bustled around the room with boiling water and clean linen cloths.

"The duchess is having a baby, Your Grace, now," the older man stated, "I'm going to move you a little, Duchess, to help you give birth. I will also need to examine you."

Millie nodded, sitting up when two maids placed several cushions behind her back to prop her up. Tatum was having none of that. He pushed the pillows out of the way and kneeled behind her, holding her as she sank against his chest.

"I have you, darling," he whispered against her ear.

She nodded but did not answer. The doctor moved to examine Millie, and a small smile spread across his mouth. "The duchess is ready to push, Your Grace," he stated, kneeling at the end of the bed.

"Push?" Tatum and Millie said in unison.

"Yes, you may push on the next contraction, Your Grace. I will tell you when you need to pause."

Millie mumbled something unintelligible under her breath but did not disagree. Tatum took a cooling cloth from a maid and dabbed it against her forehead, removing the light sheen of sweat. "There is another upon me," she gasped.

And then he felt his wife stiffen and tense in his arms. Through his body, he felt the force that she wielded to push out their child. The doctor nodded. Talked to her in a soothing, calm voice, directing her when to push and when to breathe.

Tatum held her tight, urging her to keep going. To push harder. "You're doing marvelous, my love," he said, pressing forward when she pressed back.

"That's it, Your Grace. I can see the head," the doctor informed them.

He heard Millie half-gasp, half-sob at the doctor's words and the almighty push she gave when instructed.

The next several minutes were a blur, but

looking upon his wife, watching life be birthed, was one moment in time he would never forget.

Tatum swallowed the lump in his throat as their child was hoisted into the air by the doctor and placed on Millie's stomach.

"You have a son, Your Graces," the doctor said.

Tatum could hear the joy in the doctor's voice. He reached over Millie, touching their boy's small cheek. "He is beautiful, Millie," he said.

Millie nodded, her hands too busy inspecting their baby.

"Doctor, something is not right," Millie gasped, wincing in pain yet again.

A maid took the baby, and the doctor returned to his place at the end of the bed, reaching out to inspect Millie a second time. His eyes met Tatum's over Millie's stomach, and he read the shock within them.

"There is another baby, Your Graces," he stated.

"Two," Millie and Tatum said in unison.

Millie clutched for Tatum's hand, squeezing his digits to the point that he fought not to yell himself.

"I cannot do it again. It hurts so much," she said.

But they did not have long to wait. Within a

minute of their first child, a second was born, a girl as pretty and full-lipped as her mama.

"A daughter, Your Graces," the doctor stated, checking Millie first before stepping away from the bed to give them privacy. "I do believe there are no more," he said.

Tatum felt Millie relax in his arms, and she glanced over her shoulder, meeting his eye. "Two. We have two babies," she said, awe in her voice, laughter in her eyes.

He nodded, staring in disbelief as their son was placed in Millie's hold. Two bundles, a future duke and lady. They were blessed indeed.

"I'm so relieved you are well, my darling. How marvelous you are," he said, unable to believe what she had accomplished or what had occurred.

Two!

She chuckled. "My mother will not know what to do with herself when visiting. We must surprise everyone, let it be a shock to them as much as us," she said.

He smiled. "I couldn't agree more."

LATER THAT EVENING, TATUM PACED their room, rocking his daughter in his arms while their son fed from Millie. Duchess or not, his wife had refused a wet nurse and wanted to provide for her children for as long as she could.

Of course, the wet nurse was never far away, nor were the nannies they had hired, and he would ensure Millie gained her rest and healed after gifting him two precious children.

"What should we call them, my love?" he asked, coming to sit beside her on the bed.

She took in the children, a small wistful smile on her lips. Never had she appeared so beautiful to him. How he adored her. "Hmm, I do not know. Do we want matching names?" she asked.

Tatum frowned, unsure. "I will let you choose, my love. After watching you today, I will never deny you anything again," he stated, meaning every word.

She chuckled. "I love Alexander, and we could name our daughter Alexandria. What do you think of those names?" she asked him.

He took in their children, their small button noses and long, dark lashes. "I think that suits them very well," he agreed.

Their son fell asleep during his feed and lay in Millie's lap, a contented little fellow if ever he saw. "They are beautiful, Millie. Thank you for being my wife, making a family with me."

Millie reached over to him, clasping his jaw. "I think these little sweethearts were a joint endeavor. I adore our little family too," she said, kissing him softly.

"I cherish you," he added, meeting her gaze.

"When we first met, I hazard you did not

think you would ever say such things about me and certainly did not think I would one day be your wife."

He thought back to the house party in Surrey and their first disagreement over the oldest horse race in England. "No, I never thought I would be so fortunate to have you beside me in life, but I'm so glad you cannot count. None of this may have happened should you have learned your numbers better."

She gasped and shoved against him with her shoulder. "Who says I did not count incorrectly on purpose," she teased, wiggling her brows.

Tatum threw back his head and laughed, startling both babies. "I would not doubt such a ruse, Duchess. After today I know you're capable of great things."

"Yes," she wistfully sighed, glancing back at their children. "I am, aren't I?"

Yes, she was.

Dear Reader,

Thank you for taking the time to read *One Day my Duke Will Come*! I hope you enjoyed the fifth book in my Wayward Woodvilles series!

I'm forever grateful to my readers, and if you're able, I would appreciate an honest review of *One Day my Duke Will Come*. As they say, feed an author, leave a review!

Alternatively, you can keep in contact with me by visiting my website, subscribing to my newsletter or following me online. You can contact me at www.tamaragill.com.

Tamara Gill

Don't Miss Tamara's Other Romance Series

The Wayward Yorks

A Wager with a Duke

My Reformed Rogue

Wild, Wild, Duke

The Wayward Woodvilles

A Duke of a Time

On a Wild Duke Chase

Speak of the Duke

Every Duke has a Silver Lining

One Day my Duke Will Come

Surrender to the Duke

My Reckless Earl

Brazen Rogue

The Notorious Lord Sin

Wicked in My Bed

Royal House of Atharia

To Dream of You

A Royal Proposition

Forever My Princess

Only an Earl Will Do

Only a Duke Will Do

Only a Viscount Will Do

Only a Marquess Will Do

Only a Lady Will Do

A Time Traveler's Highland Love

To Conquer a Scot

To Save a Savage Scot

To Win a Highland Scot

A Stolen Season

A Stolen Season

A Stolen Season: Bath

A Stolen Season: London

Scandalous London

A Gentleman's Promise

A Captain's Order

A Marriage Made in Mayfair

High Seas & High Stakes

His Lady Smuggler

Her Gentleman Pirate

A Wallflower's Christmas Wreath

ABOUT THE AUTHOR

Tamara is an Australian author who grew up in an old mining town in country South Australia, where her love of history was founded. So much so, she made her darling husband travel to the UK for their honeymoon, where she dragged him from one historical monument and castle to another.

A mother of three, her two little gentlemen in the making, a future lady (she hopes) keep her busy in the real world, but whenever she gets a moment's peace she loves to write romance novels in an array of genres, including regency, medieval and time travel.